W9-BCB-188

"You're quite safe," she told him calmly

"I got the message the first time," Christy added. "I know you don't desire me."

"Now where did you get that idea, I wonder," Simon mused. "I simply said I didn't want to marry you."

His words came as too much of a shock. "But you rejected me!" she reminded him.

Simon took hold of her arms and stared down at her. He looked grim and angry. "You came to my room prepared to barter your virginity for a wedding ring," he stated flatly. "*That* was what I rejected."

She had hoped that once he had made love to her he would want to marry her, Christy acknowledged. But she had never intended using her virginity as a lever. She thought of telling him as much, then changed her mind. What was the point?

Books by Penny Jordan

HARLEQUIN PRESENTS

HARLEQUIN SIGNATURE EDITION

These books may be available at your local bookseller.

Don't miss any of our special offers. Write to us at the following address for information on our newest releases.

Harlequin Reader Service
P.O. Box 52040, Phoenix, AZ 85072-2040
Canadian address: P.O. Box 2800, Postal Station A,
5170 Yonge St., Willowdale, Ont. M2N 6J3

PENNY JORDAN

exorcism

Harlequin Books

TORONTO • NEW YORK • LONDON
AMSTERDAM • PARIS • SYDNEY • HAMBURG
STOCKHOLM • ATHENS • TOKYO • MILAN

Harlequin Presents first edition January 1986
ISBN 0-373-10850-8

Original hardcover edition published in 1985
by Mills & Boon Limited

Copyright © 1985 by Penny Jordan. All rights reserved.
Philippine copyright 1985. Australian copyright 1985.
Except for use in any review, the reproduction or utilization of
this work in whole or in part in any form by any electronic,
mechanical or other means, now known or hereafter invented,
including xerography, photocopying and recording, or in any
information storage or retrieval system, is forbidden without
the permission of the publisher, Harlequin Enterprises Limited,
225 Duncan Mill Road, Don Mills, Ontario, Canada M3B 3K9.

All the characters in this book have no existence outside the
imagination of the author and have no relation whatsoever to
anyone bearing the same name or names. They are not even
distantly inspired by any individual known or unknown to the
author, and all the incidents are pure invention.

The Harlequin trademarks, consisting of the words
HARLEQUIN PRESENTS and the portrayal of a Harlequin,
are trademarks of Harlequin Enterprises Limited and are
registered in the Canada Trade Marks Office; the portrayal
of a Harlequin is registered in the United States Patent
and Trademark Office.

Printed in U.S.A.

CHAPTER ONE

IT had been a perfect spring, the bright, rain-washed April days giving way to a totally unexpected lazy May heat that made the Dorset hedgerows bloom, and old Harry Carver, who came twice a month to do their garden, proclaim pessimistically that nothing good would come of it, but now May was sliding languorously into June with no sign of a break in the weather. Christy was lying on her back in the small orchard, squinting at the sky occasionally and wondering if she dare be lazy for another half an hour or whether she ought to return to the house and do some work. That was one of the pleasant aspects of working for one's mother, and having endured the rigours of a nine-to-five routine in the early days when she had just left secretarial school, Christy appreciated her present freedom all the more.

Not that her job was in any way a sinecure. Working for a compulsive writer brought its own share of crises. Her mother loathed using a dictaphone and had a habit of scribbling down her thoughts in the most unlikely places on the smallest scraps of paper she could find, and then there was always the inevitable panic when one of these 'treasures' couldn't be found.

Not many young women of twenty-four would want to work for their mothers, especially not such a successful mother as hers, Christy acknowledged, but then the images the words 'successful' in conjunction with the word 'woman' conjured up were so totally at variance with her petite, vague, sometimes infuriating, often enchanting mother.

Christy had lost count of the number of people over the years who had been lulled into a false sense of security by her mother's apparent vagueness. As a young widow with a small baby to rear and no visible means of support, other than a small pension from the Armed Services, she had somehow managed to withstand the strong pressure brought to bear by both her own and her husband's parents that she make her home with them. At twenty she was young enough to marry again they had both told her, and it was foolish to burden herself with the responsibility of a small baby when both sets of parents were willing to take over for her. Somehow she had withstood that pressure ... somehow she had carved a niche for herself in the jungle of the publishing world persevering with her children's stories until she found a publisher willing to take them.

Now, under her pen-name, she was famous, but Christy did not envy her that fame. Any artistic talents she had inherited from her mother found expression in the illustrations she did for her mother's books. And not only her mother's. Christy had a rare talent that other writers had seized on eagerly, and the royalty cheques she received for this work could have made her pleasantly independent of her mother had she had any desire to live alone.

Perhaps she *was* unusual at twenty-four in still living at home. But when 'home' was a rambling Victorian vicarage with close on two acres of delightful garden, set in a small Dorset village complete with thatched cottages; a small village store and a local pub whose food drew visitors from miles around, it seemed hard to visualise any merit in moving. She and her mother got on well and were close without stifling one another. Georgina Lawrence had always had the knack of preserving her own privacy and it was a gift she had passed on to Christy. While it would have been a fallacy to say they were as close as sisters, they were, as well as mother and daughter, friends, with some interests they shared and some they did not. Her mother was wise, Christy acknowledged, in the way that people who had suffered great emotional pain often were. She was also capable of standing back from a situation and assessing it from the outside; although she had explained to Christy that both sets of parents had been bitterly opposed to her living alone when she was widowed, she had also gone on to say that their opposition was simply a sign of their caring. All in all her mother was a very remarkable woman, and yet Christy felt no envy of her. She herself was not professionally ambitious . . . perhaps that was what was wrong with her . . . her lack of ambition. Her mother had told her that she took after her father; the young army captain who had been killed in Northern Ireland by a bomb blast.

Christy had once asked her mother why she had never married again. She knew it hadn't been for lack of offers. Even now at forty-five her mother was an extremely attractive woman; small and slim with a thick head of naturally curly dark red hair and animated feminine features.

'Perhaps because I've grown beyond it,' she had responded openly. 'I loved your father as one does at eighteen—blindly . . . passionately . . . our relationship was one of love formed between equals . . . both of us young and united against our parents. They thought we were too young to marry, and probably they were right. The danger of marrying young and then losing one's partner is that one sees the deterioration of one's peers' marriages while one's own remains perfect and inviolate. Who knows, had your father lived he might have become entrenched in the same male role I see so often in the husbands of my friends . . . he might not have wanted me to write . . . I'm a very selfish woman, Christy . . . women have to be selfish to do what they want because there are so many other pressures on them, both emotional and social. If I have not married again perhaps it is because I relish my right to make my own decisions, to do as I please. As a man's lover I retain that right and he respects me for it, as his wife, a subtle re-arrangement of priorities takes place and most men, whether they are prepared to admit it or not, want their wives to conform to a certain image. Perhaps with your generation it will be different, I don't know, but I should hate to commit myself to a relationship and then find it soured by habit and familiarity.'

Christy had understood what her mother had meant. She had looked long and hard at the marriages of her mother's friends, and realised why her mother might prefer a lover to a husband. And undoubtedly there must have been lovers, although her mother had always been discreet. There had been no procession of 'uncles' through Christy's life, and although her mother had been a loving, caring parent, she had also instilled in Christy an independence which she herself shared; a subtle reminder that both of them had rights as individuals which they must respect in themselves as well as in one another.

Earlier on in the week her mother had gone to London to see her publisher, and had decided to stay there a few days in order to do some shopping and catch up on old friends. Christy could have gone with her but had elected to remain at home. The city in the May heat was not something that appealed to her. She stretched out luxuriously and yawned. Her skin, after so many hours spent in the garden, was tanning a warm gold. In looks she was completely unlike her mother. Her gypsy dark skin and hair had been inherited from her father, her long, heavily lashed grey eyes from her maternal grandmother; her height and slenderness, like her colouring, from her father. At twenty-four, without a scrap of make-up on and her shoulder-length hair curling wildly round her face she looked more like eighteen, although those with the experience to see it would know that pain had at some time touched her and left its indelible mark, and that having once touched her, would not be allowed to do so again.

If she had one thing in common with her mother it was a shared strength of will that both cloaked skilfully. Georgina with her vagueness, and Christy with her relaxed almost lazy approach to life. Those who didn't know her well marvelled at her lack of ambition and said pityingly that no doubt it sprang from being overshadowed by her mother, but the real explanation lay simply in the fact that there was nothing in life that Christy found worth competing for. An only child, she had a deeply romantic vein to her personality and had grown up daydreaming of fairy tales; stories of valour and heroics and later, tales of bitter-sweet and indestructible love. Her mother had gently tried to warn her that life was vastly different, but she had chosen to ignore that warning— and had paid a price for it. In one brief summer she had tasted all the pleasure life could hold, but the sweetness of it had turned to acid in her mouth when she realised she had simply been living a daydream. She had been eighteen then, now she was twenty-four. She had long ago come to terms with her disillusion-ment and her memories of the man who had caused it. Now she was content to accept life for what it was ... now she did not daydream. One day perhaps she would find a pleasant man whose company she enjoyed enough to marry ... they would have children, and a placid life, but for now she was content with her life the way it was.

The sound of a car coming down the narrow lane that led to the vicarage made her get up. From the noise it was making it sounded as though it was their one and only local taxi, which meant that her mother was back.

Brushing the grass from her shorts she walked lazily towards the house. Her trips away always fired her mother into frantic bouts of work, although before she left Georgina had said that she didn't intend to start work on her next children's collection until the autumn. She had even talked about going away on holiday—something almost unheard of for her mother. Smiling to herself, Christy walked into the kitchen and filled the electric kettle.

'Marvellous—you heard Sam's car. I'm dying for a cup of tea ... London was stifling ... you were wise not to come.'

There was a note in her mother's voice that Christy picked up on but didn't respond to, concentrating instead on making the tea.

'Outside, or in the conservatory?' she asked her when she had set a small tray with cups and her mother's favourite biscuits. Neither of them had a weight problem, but both of them were sparse eaters.

'The conservatory,' Georgina replied, grimacing faintly as she added. 'You don't know how lucky you are not to have inherited my wretched Celtic skin.'

'Being pale and interesting is coming back into fashion,' Christy responded. Her mother burned at the slightest touch of the sun, the pallor of her skin emphasising the warm golden brown of her own.

'I should have called you Gypsy . . .' Georgina responded wryly, taking the tray from her and leading the way to the house's old-fashioned and delightfully overgrown conservatory. It boasted a vine that ran wild much to Harry's disgust, but which both women loved, and a profusion of other plants that Georgina spent part of each morning crooning to. It helped her to collect her thoughts, she claimed.

Following her mother barefoot, her long legs slender and brown Christy sank down into one of the comfortable, ancient chairs. Georgina raised her eyebrows slightly as she observed her daughter's bare feet. They could represent no greater contrast, Christy reflected, studying her mother's immaculate slate grey skirt and toning blouse; her silk stockings and elegant high-heeled shoes.

'No shoes?' Georgina commented. 'You could cut your feet.'

'It's healthier for them,' Christy responded with a lazy smile, 'and you know how big they are. Put them in delicate shoes like yours and I'd look like an elephant.'

It wasn't true and they both knew it. Christy could, when she wanted to, look supremely elegant; she wasn't her mother's daughter for nothing, but she preferred not to copy, instead developing her own style; her clothes casual and comfortable.

Sipping her tea Georgina studied her daughter covertly. Had she done the right thing in teaching her to be independent and self-reliant . . .? Christy had a vulnerability she herself had never possessed; underneath her indolent exterior she hid emotions and uncertainties that tortured only those who possessed natures that were both romantic and idealistic. Never a joiner, Christy's individuality had become more marked over the years. A distinctly attractive young woman she seemed to prefer to be alone rather than out dating. Georgina sighed. How inconvenient the mothering instinct was; and after all the time she had put in teaching Christy to respect her own privacy and that of others, she herself could scarcely now intrude, and question. She put her cup down quickly, unaware that her daughter's quick eye had picked up on the betraying uncertainty of her movements.

'Okay, spill it out,' Christy commanded laconically. 'You've got to produce three new books by autumn, is that it?'

When her mother didn't respond, Christy frowned. 'There *is* something, I know. Please tell me . . .'

Putting down her cup, Georgina said quietly, 'Darling, Simon's back.'

Christy was proud of her lack of reaction. Not even her expressive grey eyes were allowed to mirror any feelings.

'Returning in triumph no doubt after the success of his American tour. Mum, I'm not eighteen any more,' she added gently, 'Simon Jardine means nothing to me now other than a bad memory. I'm glad for his sake that he's found success at last—he wanted it so badly, he'd never have been satisfied with anything less.' Restless, energetic Simon whom she had met six years ago, and who had stolen her unwary, foolish heart. He had told her then that nothing was more important to him than his writing and she, foolishly, had not believed him. He had just had his first book accepted by her mother's publishers; a blend of fact and fiction that made compulsive reading. Now he was a world-renowned author with three books to his name, all of them bestsellers. He had been out of the country for the last four years, either writing, or doing promotional tours, with only brief visits to the UK, mainly to see his publishers. Now, according to her mother, he was back. So what was she expected to do? Disintegrate into a thousand broken pieces?

'Don't look at me like that,' she chided her mother, pouring each of them a cup of tea. Her own senses relayed to her the disturbing information that her pulse was racing, her stomach muscles knotting in remembered tension. 'Okay, so I had a childish crush on Simon when I was eighteen—everyone's entitled to one mistake.' She managed to produce a wry smile. 'Cheer up Mum, it's not the end of the world.'

She hadn't always thought that. At eighteen, her daydreams and folly cruelly exposed by Simon's

sophisticated mockery of her, she had thought her
world *had* ended; she had *wanted* it to end, unable to
endure the pain of his cruelty ... and he had been
cruel ... encouraging her to believe he returned her
feelings only to turn on her with ill-concealed
contempt ... taunting her for her inexperience. It had
been a hard lesson for her to learn, especially as she
had made no attempt to hide her feelings from him.

'Well then, I'm afraid there's something else I must
tell you.'

Her heart seemed to seize up, her body freezing and
yet burning at the same time. Dear God don't let her
mother tell her he was married ... in love with
someone else ... 'Jeremy wants you to spend the
summer working for him.'

It was several minutes before she could take in the
meaning of her mother's words, so great was the shock
to her system of her overwhelming reaction. For years
she had barely given Simon a thought. She had put
him behind her, and yet the very mention of his name;
the very thought of him being involved with someone
else ... Just reaction, she assured herself shakily ...
Of course she was over him ... what she had felt for
him had been an adolescent crush, nothing more.

'*Jeremy* wants me to work for him?' she repeated,
trying to force her brain to work as she fought for
control of her rioting emotions.

'No, darling, not for *him*,' her mother corrected
patiently, 'He wants you to work for Simon.
Apparently, his latest book is going to be set in the
Carribean. It's about an Elizabethan adventurer who
sailed with Drake and then turned pirate. Simon
discovered a vague story about him when he was on

holiday there last year. Apparently there's a local legend about this man, and the dynasty he founded. He died in a shipwreck, apparently caused deliberately . . . the local legend is that it happened because a rival pirate gang had raided his home. Simon has worked out where such a wreck would be, if indeed the story is true, and he needs an experienced secretary, cum illustrator, cum diver to work with him during the summer while he tries to piece the story together.'

'Why me?'

Her eyes were guarded, cool almost as she studied her mother.

'I promise you it wasn't my idea. Jeremy mentioned you first. He told Simon what an excellent job you did for Miles in India last year.'

Christy sighed. Last year she had spent four months in India with Miles Trent, another writer involved with the same publishing house as her mother. Miles had been writing a novel about the British Raj and had persuaded Christy to go to India with him as his assistant. A mild-mannered, chronically disorganised man, he had claimed that the speed with which his novel had been completed was due solely to Christy's help. It was Christy's personal view that the reason Miles had been so pleased with her had little to do with her professional ability, but a good deal to do with the fact that she was completely immune to his rather film-starish brand of blond good looks. Poor Miles; no one could be less equipped to deal with the feminine interest he aroused then he was. He looked every inch the blond macho hero, but in reality was an extremely serious writer, dedicated to his work—a bachelor still at thirty-odd, he had leaned heavily on

Christy for protection from the many women who had tried to get involved with him. He was very fond of Christy but Georgina had been very frank in the opinion she gave to Christy which was that Miles was a man with little enjoyment of his effect on the opposite sex, and therefore unlikely to be very rewarding as a lover. Christy was inclined to think that her mother was right, and it had amused her when she came home to see the headlines in the gossip press, linking her name with his, and suggesting coyly that there was more than a working relationship between them. Two more unlikely lovers it would be harder to find, she had reflected at the time.

'Well, there's no need to worry about it,' she told her mother calmly now. 'Simon is hardly likely to want me as his research assistant. Why settle for a person who can combine all three roles in one, when he can have the variety of three separate females to choose from. You know Simon; he always did prefer variety.'

'I'm afraid on this occasion it seems that he doesn't,' Georgina replied quietly. 'He wants *you* to work for him, Christy. In fact he made a point of telling me so. Apparently, the timing of the diving is very important ... the weather will only be suitable for a very short span of time.'

'Tell him I can't swim,' Christy retorted curtly, 'I don't want the job Mum ... I'm looking forward to my summer off.'

'Christy ...' Georgina looked at her daughter helplessly. How could she trespass into her daughter's privacy when she was the one who had taught her to respect it in herself and others? 'My dear, I'm afraid he's determined to have you . . .'

It was an unfortunate choice of words, and one that made Christy's grey eyes glitter.

'He intends to come down here to see you. I simply could not put him off . . . If you refuse to see him he'll . . .'

'Assume that I'm still suffering from a massive adolescent crush,' Christy supplied bitterly. 'Well, I can't see why I should allow myself to be pressurised into accepting a job I don't want, simply to prove something I don't care about to someone I'm not interested in.'

'Well if that's how you feel . . .'

Georgina sounded so helpless and vague that Christy stared at her suspiciously. She knew her mother when she used that tone of voice, it meant she was concealing something.

'Obviously you don't agree with my decision.'

'My dear, it isn't a matter of not agreeing,' Georgina said gently, 'it's more a matter of why you're so determined not to agree. If you really do feel nothing towards Simon I can't see why you're refusing to accept the job. Only the other month you were saying you'd love to go to the Caribbean, but you couldn't see how you could afford it.'

'That was for a holiday—not to work, and you're right, I'm not indifferent to Simon,' she said crisply. 'I dislike him. We wouldn't work in harmony together.'

'Well, you know your own mind, but I suspect that Simon will try to change it for you. This book means a lot to him, Christy. He's done all the ground work and all he needs to do now is to make this trip out to the Caribbean.'

'And of course nothing must stand in the way of what the great Simon Jardine wants,' Christie said bitterly. 'I've been used as a sacrifice on the altar of his ambition once Mum, I'm not letting it happen again.'

After that the subject was allowed to drop. Her mother went upstairs to unpack and Christy wandered back into the garden to enjoy the last of the afternoon sun, but found that she could not settle or relax. Of course she had made the right decision, Simon Jardine had hurt her badly once, so badly that the scars still had the power to ache, but she wasn't vulnerable to him any longer. So why was she refusing? Forcing herself to be honest with herself, she acknowledged that if the job had meant working with someone else, Miles for instance, she would have jumped at it. Was she indifferent to Simon? Of course not; how could she be? He had hurt her deeply and of course she was wary, but that didn't mean she still had a crush on him—far from it. She mulled the matter over in her mind, convinced that she had made the right decision. In that summer she was eighteen she had lived on the edge of her emotions all the time. She didn't want that again. She was safe now and she enjoyed her safety, she didn't want to have to be constantly on edge, constantly reinforcing her immunity to him. And Simon himself would never accept her indifference; he was the sort of man who demanded by right the interest of every woman who crossed his path, no matter whether he was prepared to return that interest or not.

Forget about him, she scolded herself, put him out of your mind ... concentrate instead on the summer ahead. She closed her eyes, letting her thoughts drift, but annoyingly they drifted back in time not forward. At last unable to fight the crushing pressure of her memories any longer she gave up the battle. Oh very well ... perhaps she ought to remember ... perhaps she ought to relive those days again, if only mentally ... a sort of mental spring-cleaning in effect.

She had been just eighteen and attending secretarial college, looking much as she did now, although then her movements had been coltish and uncertain, her face eager, mobile, all her emotions visible in her eyes.

Her mother had been in London for over a week and she had telephoned to say she was bringing guests back with her—her publisher and a new writer who was joining the firm. Christy hadn't been particularly concerned. She had known Jeremy Thomas since she was five years old and this wasn't the first time Georgina had brought visitors down to the vicarage.

She had been in the orchard when they arrived, deeply engrossed in a book. She hadn't bothered to get up, knowing that Mrs Carver, who came in from the village once a week to clean, was there, on hand to offer the arrivals a welcome and sustenance. She would go in later when the bustle was over. She would have had to change to meet them anyway, and she wasn't in the mood. Her shorts were grubby with grass stains, white and brief, a sign that at eighteen she was still growing; her T-shirt clinging to her taut breasts. At eighteen she was vaguely embarrassed by her body; so alien to her after years spent looking at the petite femininity of her mother. Voluptuous and sexy was how her mother described her, slightly teasingly, and at eighteen she was too young to feel entirely at home with a body that drew admiring male eyes of all ages. She squirmed a little in the long grass remembering the overt stares of the few boys she knew. Always slightly shy she had made few friends at college; most of the other girls were slightly withdrawn, as unable to cope with her open sexuality as she was herself.

She was lying on her stomach, too deeply engrossed in her book to be aware of anything else, when someone bent over her to read the printed page, his voice husky, and entirely male, infusing the words she was reading with a sexuality that her own unawakened mind had not entirely absorbed. Her immediate reaction had been to snap the book closed and roll over to glare angrily at the intruder. She hated anyone coming between her and her involvement with whatever she was reading. She was still at an age where it was easy to cast aside her own person a and slip into that of the heroine and by reading as he had done the intruder had taken on the role of hero, and his voice had stroked her skin as dexterously as the hand of any lover, causing a reaction inside her that made her tense and coil, like a wary cat.

'At your age you should be experiencing romance, not reading about it,' he had mocked, his clever, masculine mouth curling faintly. Tall, taller by far than most of the men she knew, he seemed to blot out the sun with shoulders so powerfully broad that she automatically flinched away from the sheer sexuality of him. Dressed in faded jeans and a checked shirt, he was so intensely masculine that Christy, unused to such maleness, automatically recoiled from it.

His eyes had gone from her face to her body, studying her in a way that brought a wave of hot colour to her skin. Where his glance lingered, it seemed almost physically to touch. She could almost feel the explorative drift of his fingers against her skin, and she had shivered violently, hearing his soft laugh.

'So you are Georgina's "gypsy",' he had said slowly, 'a wild and passionate little savage indeed . . . I wonder how long it would take to tame you.'

She had stood up almost violently; angry at his intrusion and yet strangely excited by him. His hair was even darker than hers, blue black with a silky sheen, his skin faintly olive. His eyes which she had expected to be dark were a strange metallic gold; amber almost and she had stared curiously into them, forgetting her anger as she registered their slow appraisal.

'Definitely not your mother's daughter,' he had said at last. And for some curious reason she had felt intensely hurt; as though in some way she did not measure up to a standard he had set her. It was the first time she had ever wished she was like Georgina. Was this man her mother's lover?

He was younger than Georgina, perhaps somewhere in his mid-twenties, although it was hard to tell, and yet even her innocence could not protect her from being aware of his intense sexuality. It wasn't that he was outstandingly good looking; his features were almost too hard for that, his jaw and chin stubbornly unyielding; his cheekbones high, thrusting against his tanned skin, his nose faintly crooked as though it might have once been broken; but there was something about him that made her want to stare and go on staring. He stretched his hand out to her, grasping her wrist with lean fingers. Their touch was cool and yet where they circled her skin it seemed to burn like fire.

'Georgina sent me to get you . . . It seems you and I are to play together like good children while she and Jeremy discuss work. Do you think we can do that, Christy?' he had asked her mockingly, 'Do you think we can play nicely together?'

She had known instinctively then that he and her mother were not lovers, and in her pitiable innocence had not realised the danger the joy that knowledge brought, represented. She had looked into his amber eyes and had felt suddenly as though for the first time in her life she was truly alive. He had smiled down at her, a curious smile tinged with a knowledge she could only guess at. And that was how it had started.

'Christy?'

Hearing her mother call her name brought her out of the past, so abruptly that she still carried its residue of pain with her as she made her way back to the house. She had thought reliving what had happened might have a cathartic effect, but perhaps for that she needed to relive every event . . . every moment of that brief summer.

CHAPTER TWO

'I'M going up now, how about you?'

Christy shook her head lightly, 'I'm not tired enough yet.'

She wasn't relaxed enough to sleep; that was the truth of the matter. Although it had not been mentioned during dinner, she knew her mother still felt she should accept the job with Simon. Sighing, Christy went over to the record cabinet and selected a recording of some Handel. His music, always so relaxing, would surely help to unravel her knotted muscles and induce a desire to sleep.

Curling up in an armchair, she closed her eyes and let the sounds wash over her. Her mother's room wasn't directly above the sitting room and so it wouldn't disturb her.

Simon had been faintly mocking about her love of classical music. 'You want everything to be so romantic, don't you?' he had taunted her . . . 'but life isn't like that, gypsy.' He had bought her other records; some pop, some classical . . . all of them containing the message that life comprised pain as well as pleasure. Her mother and Jeremy had been deeply involved in working out the details of her schedule for the coming autumn; there was an American tour to be fitted in as well as two new books, and there were also several other matters they had to discuss, so that Simon and Christy were thrown very much into one

another's company. She had finished at college for the
summer, and in the early days she and Simon had
made good use of the Vicarage's rather ancient tennis
court.

He was a demanding opponent, who never willingly
let her win, and sometimes his driving desire to win
angered her. She herself cared little about winning or
losing and somehow he made her feel that this was a
lack in her.

'So unambitious,' he had taunted her one day.
'What do you plan to do with your life, Christy? Fall
in love, get married and live happily ever after?'

He had laughed at her scarlet cheeks but his
laughter had not held any amusement, rather it had
had the hard edge of a man made bitter by contempt.

'What a trap for my sex, Mother Nature has
designed in you. Your looks and your body promise so
much ... offer so much enticement, and yet they
cannot be had without the payment of a price can
they, my gypsy? And that price is marriage.'

She hadn't understood his anger; not then. She had
simply thought he was mocking her and had not
understood why. The frustration which someone with
more experience might have recognised, was hidden
from her by her own innocence.

She could vividly remember the first time he
kissed her. He had taken her out for the day in his
car—a small sports model; brightly scarlet. When
she had admired it, he had laughed, faintly
disparagingly.

'It's a young man's car, something he buys before
he commits himself to marriage and a family, and the
inevitable saloon, but that's not for me, Christy,' he

had told her, 'my choice of car will always only have room for the one passenger.'

He had taken her down to the coast, and with her directions had found the sheltered, almost secret little beach she often went to with her mother. She had been wearing her swimsuit under her jeans but had felt shiveringly self-conscious about taking them off, sitting tense and curiously breathless as he removed his shirt and his own jeans. Her lack of father or brothers had not left her with any particular curiosity about the male form. There had been all the usual girlish giggled confidences at school, and her mother had matter-of-factly outlined the intimacies shared by male and female when she was old enough to understand them. There had never been any undue embarrassment between mother and daughter, and Georgina had been frank and explicit with her in their discussions about sex. Even so there was something vastly different about knowing what went to make up the male anatomy and then seeing the reality of it, barely concealed by brief black swimming shorts. Simon's soft laugh when he realised she was looking at him had reduced her to a mass of guilty blushes, quickly turning her head aside, but not quickly enough apparently. He had turned it back, holding her face between his hands, his palms hard and warm against her skin.

'There's nothing wrong in wanting to look at me, Christy,' he told her then. 'I enjoy looking at you you know . . . I do it all the time . . . in fact, I want to do more than look at you. Much more,' Christy had thought she heard him mutter thickly under his breath as his head descended, blotting out the sun, his mouth

moving slowly over hers until her lips lost their
stiffness and clung softly to his with shy eagerness.

He had groaned slightly as he ended the kiss, still
holding her face as he asked in a rasping voice, 'I
suppose you're still a virgin?'

Christy had nodded her head, worried because her
confirmation did not seem to please him. Surely all
men wanted the girl they fell in love with to be
virginal . . . untouched . . . and Simon must love her,
even though he hadn't said so . . . otherwise why
would he have kissed her? Made suddenly brave by
the heady pleasure of knowing he cared about her, she
had reached out and traced the line of his mouth with
her fingers, and had said softly, 'Don't let it worry you
. . . it isn't important.'

What she had meant was that it wasn't important to
her . . . She didn't mind being virginal; in fact there
was no one she would rather have to initiate her into
the mysteries of love than Simon. Strange, how she
had known the moment he kissed her that she loved
him and that he returned her love; and how knowing
that had made everything else drop into place . . . Now
she could understand why her pulses thudded every
time she saw him; why her stomach tensed and her
skin coloured hotly.

She hadn't said anything else, simply smiling shyly
at Simon, but his topaz eyes had glittered over her face
and then her body and she had felt the tension in his
fingers, threatening to crush the fragile bones of her
face before he released her to say huskily, 'Come on,
race you into the water.'

Christy was a strong swimmer. It was her favourite
sport and she had learned to dive very young. During

her final two years at school she had taken advantage of living near the coast to join a sea-diving school, quickly learning to love exploring the underwater environment.

Simon, too, was a strong swimmer, and when she realised that she was not going to be able to beat him she dived quickly, swimming underwater, holding her breath. She was almost at the limit of her lung power when Simon dived down alongside her, grasping her roughly and hauling her to the surface. They broke the water together, mischief darkening her eyes, fury darkening his, as he grasped her, treading water as he shook her roughly.

'Just what the hell were you playing at?' he demanded thickly, 'when I looked round and couldn't see you...' One hand was curled through her wet hair, imprisoning her, the other round her waist and she could feel the hectic thud of his heart. He was angry because he loved her, she marvelled, almost giddy with the sudden sensation of joy. It made her brave—and foolish. Pressing herself against him, she kissed his wet throat. 'I'm sorry...'

His skin pulsed beneath her mouth, a fierce tension emanating from him, his voice unexpectedly rough as he said thickly, 'So you damned well ought to be. I'm not a man who likes to be teased, Christy,' he warned her, disengaging himself from her. Tawny lights flickered in his eyes, inciting a fierce heat in her veins, as she sensed that he wasn't simply talking about her dive.

'You're the one who teases me.' She made a small mou, touching her tongue to her salt-encrusted lips. 'I wouldn't know how to tease you even if I wanted to.'

She knew that she was lying, and the delicious, heady feeling of power racing through her body ensured that she didn't care.

'You're a woman, aren't you?' Simon's voice was still thick, but now it was underlined with a vague derision that chilled her. As they swam back to shore she pushed it aside. Simon loved her; she knew that ... It could only be a matter of time before he asked her to marry him. As she walked across the hot sand she remembered that she had heard him say on more than one occasion that he had no intention of tying himself down, but that was before he had fallen in love with *her*, she had assured herself comfortably. Of course he would want to marry her. They could find somewhere to live locally; Simon would write, and she would be his devoted wife. She preened herself mentally, seeing herself in three or four years to come ... a baby ... perhaps even two ... Simon ... and a placid, happy existence ...

Dear God, Christy thought, groaning to herself as the music stopped. What a naïve idiot she had been. Anyone less cut out for domestic bliss than Simon would have been impossible to find. But all the guilt wasn't hers. Yes, she had been foolish to delude herself into believing that Simon wanted to marry her, but he had had the experience, even then, to know what was happening to her. He could surely have gently but firmly nipped her feelings in the bud then, instead of letting them flower ... instead of encouraging them to flower, and then savagely destroying her? She saw with hindsight that it was almost as though he had hated her, and yet why? All she had been guilty of was falling in love with him.

She had not chased him; she hadn't had the experience for that, and if he had not kissed her . . . touched her . . . she would surely never have realised how she felt about him. But he had kissed her . . . and touched her . . .

After their swim they had sunbathed. Christy, already healthily tanned, had not bothered to cover herself with any cream. She didn't need it, but Simon had insisted that he did—a ploy which she should have recognised immediately for what it was.

Willingly she had taken the plastic bottle he gave her, pouring a little of the oil into her palm while he lay on his stomach his head lying on his forearms. She had kneeled beside him, spreading the oil carefully across his shoulders, stroking it in with fingertips that soon became blissfully addicted to the sensation of warm male skin beneath them. Her whole body seemed to tingle as she worked her way over his back, and then at his insistence, his legs. The sensation of the fine dark hairs beneath her fingers was an unfamiliar one, and yet strangely exciting, her pulses reacting as violently as a fairground dipper ride. The pressure of Simon's hand on her thigh as he raised himself up on his side made her insides melt in a curious surge of heat.

'Now my chest,' he commanded softly, and although she had begun to tell him that it was pointless oiling his chest since she had just done his back, the words died unspoken, as he cupped her hands together, and poured the oil into them, guiding her palms against his skin.

The boys she had seen on the beach did not have bodies like Simon's. It was hard and entirely masculine shadowed by dark body hair which she had always mentally thought distasteful when seen on men on television or films, but which now when touched unleashed a deep-seated excitement that made her insides churn. She had reached his waist before Simon stopped her, pulling her down into his arms, covering her mouth with his own, while it was still parted in a rounded 'oh' of surprise.

'No, don't close it,' he muttered to her, stroking her lips with his tongue, and biting gently at her lower one until her senses were inflamed completely beyond her ability to control.

Her mind registered the husky timbre of his voice when he said softly, 'I don't think you need this do you?' his hands sliding down the straps of her swimsuit, but until she felt the harsh rasp of his body hair against her breasts she wasn't aware of their import, and by then it was too late to protest—she no longer wanted to do so. Her breasts, so full and firm; and always secretly slightly resented in her own heart of hearts, because they were so blatantly curvaceous, seemed to have been designed especially to fill Simon's hands. Under his skilled caress she felt them swell slightly, her nipples so tight and hard that they almost hurt. It was a totally unexpected sensation, something she had read about but never realised could be completely devastating. She made a small sound at the back of her throat, and as though he understood what she was feeling, Simon had gentled her with soft murmurs, stretching his body so that she was pressed along the length of it. 'I know ... I know ...' he whispered huskily, 'Feel what you're doing to me, too.'

The fiercely aroused throb of his body against hers was exciting and yet frightening too. Wild emotions clutched at the pit of her stomach making her ache to move closer to him, to explore the pleasures she had read about and not as yet experienced for herself.

But when Simon made a harsh sound in his throat and bent his head to tug fiercely on her nipple with a mouth that seemed to burn into her skin, fear overcame desire and Christy flinched back from him, unable to cope with the emotions threatening to overwhelm her. She wanted him to make love to her, but the suppressed violence she sensed in him frightened her. When she visualised him making love to her, it was in some romantic setting ... on their honeymoon, when he would be a tender, considerate lover ... not this driven, almost angry man, who was pushing her swimsuit straps back, and glowering at her darkly, his eyes burning as fierce a gold as the dying sun. She reached out to touch him and he jerked away saying harshly, 'For God's sake don't make it worse than it is ... Let's get back before I really do something I'll regret.'

His words had made her unhappy, but only for a little while. It was natural that he should be angry, she reasoned with herself. Obviously he regretted his lack of self-control. Loving her, he must respect her ... and of course, he wouldn't want to make love to her until they were married.

Opening her eyes, Christy groaned. How naïve and smug she had been. In reality Simon had been very far from loving her and had in fact, merely desired her. His anger had sprung from nothing more than simple frustration but she had not had the wit to see it, and so she had gone on building her ridiculous fairy castles in the air, sublimely unaware of the fragility of their foundations.

If her mother had not been so busy she might have realised sooner what was happening, but even if she had, Christy doubted that she would have realised her daughter's foolish dreams. Christy had never been encouraged by her own mother to believe that marriage, a family and home should automatically be a woman's goal in life; no, it was her own unrealistically romantic nature that had led her down that particular garden path. For all that she had known of the physical aspects of sex, she had known nothing of its sheer power . . . of its intensity, or that a man and woman could simply be drawn together by it in a relationship which had nothing to do with love.

Simon had made some attempt to warn her, she supposed, looking at it from his point of view. Before they left the beach he had turned to her and demanded sombrely, 'You do know what it is that I want from you don't you, Christy?'

And she, believing he meant that he wanted her love, replied dreamily, 'Yes, and I want it too . . .' Not realising that in his eyes she had committed herself to a sexual relationship with him that he had no intention of making anything more than extremely fleeting. All the evidence had been there; she had simply blinded herself to it, seeing only what she wanted to see, deceiving herself until it was impossible to deceive herself any longer; until Simon had simply been forced to tell her the truth; that he did not love her; never had loved her and had not the slightest intention of marrying her. Far from it!

Sighing, she roused herself and switched off the record player, making her way to bed.

It was ironic to think that sexually she was very little more experienced now than she had been then, although of course now she was much more aware of her body's reactions and capabilities. There had been times when she had almost wished she could meet a man she simply desired physically. Someone who could release her body from its virginal bondage but thus far that had not happened, and as the years slipped by her virginity itself became something of a problem. She felt it was slightly ridiculous to be sexually unawakened at twenty-four, and often wondered wryly why nature had been unkind enough to burden the female race with a barrier that proclaimed its own truths and untruths. As she went up to bed she reassured herself that she had made the right decision in refusing to work for Simon. She wasn't eighteen any more, ready to drop everything to run at his bidding. Let him look elsewhere for his assistance; if the gossip columns she read were only half right, it shouldn't prove too strenuous a task.

She woke up early, watching the sun stretch lazy golden fingers through her window and knew it was going to be another fine day. She lay in bed, closing her eyes, basking in the heat coming through the glass—a deceptive heat; as deceptive as Simon's feelings for her.

She could recognise now with maturity that the tense moods that had gripped him during that long ago summer had sprung from sexual frustration. Then she had been alternatively frightened and thrilled by them, skittish as a young foal, shying away from his touch while she entreated it. Images of Simon as he had been then danced behind her closed eyelids; Simon in tennis shorts and T-shirt, his skin bronzed and male; Simon in jeans, powerful and lithe as he worked in the garden and then most potent of all, Simon the night after they had had their quarrel.

She couldn't remember how it had started; it had sprung up quickly like a summer thunder storm. Her mother had gone away to see a friend who had suddenly been taken into hospital and Jeremy had gone with her. She and Simon were alone in the house. His moods had grown worse and uncertain of him, wanting confirmation that he still loved her, she had used her mother's absence to confront him that evening, going up to him and twining her arms round his neck, silently begging for his kiss. He had jerked away from her she remembered and had then come back to her, kissing her with an angry hunger that half-shocked her, releasing her to demand thickly, 'What is it you want from me, Christy? This?' He had kissed her again, forcing her mouth to part, infusing her with an intense heat as his hands moved seductively over her body. She was trembling when he released her she remembered. 'Or is there a price attached to your love? Is it me you want ... really me ...'

'You know I love you,' she had cried out. She had seen the change in his expression when she mentioned the word 'love' but had not understood it—then!

'Then come to bed with me now,' he had responded thickly. 'Come and show me how much you love me.'

She had hesitated, tense and unsure of him all of a sudden. 'What's the matter?' he had demanded harshly, his eyes derisive. 'Are you sure it's me you're in love with or simply the idea of being in love . . .? Is it *me* you want, Christy, or simply marriage, because I'm telling you now that marriage simply does not figure in my plans. I've got far too much living to do to tie myself down to one woman,' he had told her brutally. 'If you want to be part of that living then fine, but I can't offer you permanency . . .'

She hadn't been able to believe her ears. 'You don't want me,' she had cried out childishly in pain.

'Oh I want you all right.' Simon's voice had been curt, hard; his topaz eyes glittering hotly over her skin.

'But I love you.'

He had laughed then, a harsh bitter sound. 'What you feel isn't *love*,' he had told her with cruel astringency. 'It's physical desire, pure and simple. You haven't the experience to love anyone, you're still little more than a baby. Too frightened to live life alone . . . wanting marriage as a security blanket.'

She had cried out in anguish, hating him for what he was saying to her; for what he was doing to her fragile daydreams. She hadn't been aware of him walking away, only of her pain.

The next day she had gone out of her way to avoid him, but that night, driven by the tension inside herself, she had gone to his room after he had gone to bed. He had been lying on his side, his skin exposed where he had kicked the bedclothes aside. She had caught her breath at the sight of him, tears stinging her eyes. She did love him . . . she did. She had crept nearer to the bed, stiffening when his eyes opened. For a moment they had simply looked at one another and then he had sat up, careless of the fact that he was naked. 'What the hell are you doing here?' he had demanded softly.

'I want you to make love to me.' She had said it as calmly as she could, her eyes defying him to reject her. If that was the sacrifice demanded of her to prove her love then she was prepared to make it. No doubt she had looked the complete tragic heroine, Christy reflected sardonically now, and that was doubtless the reason for the alien twist of emotion she had seen blaze momentarily in his eyes.

'Do you now.' He had pulled her down on to the bed alongside him, his hard, experienced hands dealing efficiently with her nightclothes, his eyes hooded and mysterious as he studied her trembling, naked body in the light through the open windows.

'Be still my little sacrificial lamb,' he had murmured to her as he bent towards her. 'You wanted this—remember?'

His mouth was hot and forceful on her own, his touch drugging her senses, everything else forgotten as he brought her body burningly alive. A wild elation sang in her veins; an overwhelming compulsion urging her forward.

'I hope you're remembering that this is only lust,' he had muttered the words against her mouth and instantly her blood had chilled, her eyes enormous, frozen pools of pain in her pale face.

'You really don't love me?' She had stammered the words, colour stinging her skin as he mocked.

'No, I really don't. If I take you now it will be because my body craves yours, that's all, Christy, and if you're honest, you'll admit that it's the same for you . . .'

'No!' The denial had burst past her lips as she sprang off the bed, all her desire suddenly gone, and a deep sense of humiliation taking its place. She couldn't remember finding her nightclothes or going back to her own room, but she must have done so. She had cried long into the night, muffling the sound against her pillow, not sure whom she hated the most Simon, or herself. He didn't love her at all . . . he had never love her . . .

It was only pride that enabled her to face him the following morning. She refused his invitation to play tennis, marvelling at his ability to put aside what had happened, ignoring it almost. *She* could not do so. For the remainder of the duration of his stay she had treated him with a frozen politeness, breaking down only when he had gone, pouring out her pain to her mother.

Georgina had sighed and berated herself for not realising what was happening. 'Simon is a loner, darling,' she had told her. 'He's also, unfortunately for you, an extremely sexy man. You'll get over it,' she had promised, but Christy hadn't believed her. Not then.

She had of course, but the pain of her humiliation at his hands had left a legacy that still stung. He could have let her down more easily. Realising that she was not going to go back to sleep she got up and showered.

Downstairs the house drowsed in the early morning sun. She went into the kitchen and started to prepare her mother's breakfast tray. Georgina was normally a late night person, and preferred to have breakfast in bed.

Christy was just pouring water on to the tea when

she heard the squeak of the back door. Harry didn't come on a Thursday and it wasn't Mrs Carver's day either. She turned round slowly, her nerve endings prickling warningly as her eyes met those of the man leaning against the kitchen door.

Six years had barely changed him. He was a little thinner perhaps, but his hair was still just as dark, his skin just as tanned, his eyes impossibly golden.

'Hello, Simon.'

She was pleased that her voice was so even.

'Still the devoted handmaiden I see.'

'My mother likes to have breakfast in bed, I like to get up early.' She kept her voice deliberately neutral. 'Have you come to see her?'

'No, I've come to see you, as you damn well know. Why won't you come and work for me?'

'Why should I?' She shrugged slim shoulders.

'Still not forgiven me?' His mouth twisted derisively, and anger quickened inside her. Her eyebrows arched, her eyes coolly meeting his.

'What for? Inviting me to share your bed? My dear Simon, I'm old enough now to realise what an accolade that was, especially in view of my own pathetic lack of experience.'

'Are you?' His voice was infused with mild irony. 'What are you trying to tell me, Christy? That given the choice now, you'd choose differently—lust in preference to virtue?'

'I wasn't aware that *I* did make the choice,' she replied evenly, but he confounded her by saying.

'You were scared to death of me making love to you, you simply thought that if I did I'd have no option but to marry you.'

'That's not true.' The denial was a cry of pain, her face white under her tan.

'What does it matter? It's all water under the bridge now anyway. Why won't you come to the Caribbean with me? What are you so afraid of? That I'll try to make love to you?'

'Hardly.' Her voice was extremely dry. 'In point of fact, I'm not afraid at all, Simon, simply uninterested.'

He came towards her, taking her chin between his fingers, before she could avoid him, his expression mocking as he drawled, 'Well, well, you have grown up, haven't you? And what have you been doing with yourself for the last six years?'

His voice suggested that whatever it was it couldn't have been anything of any merit and where once his cynicism would have unnerved her now it simply made her angry.

'Living well,' she told him sweetly, shaking herself free. 'Didn't you know—it *is* the best revenge.'

His mouth twisted. 'All grown up with a vengeance, aren't we? I wonder how far that sophisticated veneer goes? It might be interesting to find out.'

'Far enough to deal with men like you, Simon,' she told him coolly. 'Please stop baiting me and go and find someone else to work for you?'

'Sure you're indifferent to me?' he mocked, grasping her wrist, his thumb on her racing pulse. 'If so, prove it and come and work for me.'

'I don't have to prove it.' She gave him a tight smile.

'Come with me, and I promise I won't put your indifference to the test.'

His arrogance infuriated her. It flashed darkly in her

eyes, her mouth tightening with temper. 'Why me?' she demanded bitterly. 'God, you could have your pick.'

His mouth twisted. 'Very flattering, but I'm not prepared to pay the price. You, on the other hand, I know I'm safe with.'

'Get a male assistant if you're that scared.'

'A man probably wouldn't be prepared to cook and clean,' he told her arrogantly. 'I want to keep what I'm doing as secret as possible. I can manage the boat we'll be using single-handed, and I want as few people as possible involved. You fit the bill on every count.'

'Right down to not wanting to share your bed,' Christy seethed.

'Oh, it's not sharing my bed that worries me, it's the price I might be expected to pay for the privilege of enjoying my female companion's favours,' he returned cynically.

'Still the same old Simon.'

'But of course. *Now* will you come with me?'

'If I refuse?'

'Then perhaps I'll just stay around and see just how deep your indifference goes, gipsy.' He laughed at her expression. 'Come with me, you know in your heart-of-hearts you want to. How can staying here compare with a summer spent in the Caribbean?'

'Extremely favourably,' Christy flung at him tartly, 'especially when the Caribbean includes you.'

'But you'll come?'

His thumb was caressing her wrist and it was taking all her willpower not to respond to his insidious caress. She didn't love him; she didn't even like him very much, but her body was aware of him. He had been right, she realised with a certain wry amusement.

Lust was all it had ever been. Why shouldn't she go? It would be good to show him just how much she had changed.

She shrugged carelessly, 'Why not . . .? On the strict understanding, of course, that I am simply your assistant.'

It was his turn to shrug. 'If that's the way you want it. Was that all you were to Miles? Simply an assistant?'

His question caught her off-guard. On the point of replying truthfully she checked, and then said smoothly. 'Really Simon, I don't think my relationship with Miles is any concern of yours.'

'Not in the ordinary sense,' he agreed calmly, 'but he's in the Bahamas at the moment and it's quite conceivable that we might run into him. I ought to warn you that at the moment he's heavily involved with someone else.'

'Petra Finnegan,' Christy responded coolly. 'Yes, I do read the papers, Simon.'

'Umm. You're obviously not jealous.' His eyes searched hers with cool intent, 'but then I don't suppose he was your first lover.'

His analytical regard angered her, her voice tense as she bit out. 'What's the matter, Simon, regretting that you weren't?'

He laughed and released her. 'Hell, no. Timid little virgins weren't, and still aren't, my style, Christy. You should know that.'

She almost recoiled from the cruelty of it, but then her sense of humour came to her rescue. 'Oh I do,' she agreed softly. 'Luckily for me it's not an aversion all men share.'

There was a tense little silence that made her stomach curl in instinctive and unexpected alarm, and then Simon drawled mockingly, 'Okay, Christy, game, set and match. Now can we get down to business? I don't have much time.'

'In that case you took rather a chance, didn't you?' she responded coolly. 'What if I had refused to come with you?'

'I could have found someone else, it wouldn't have been an impossibility, but you're the assistant I want.'

'And you always get what you want, is that it?'

'I try to,' he agreed suavely. 'Now are you going to take that tray up to Georgina and break the glad tidings?'

Her mother was awake when Christy went up.

'Simon's here,' she told her crisply as she walked in. 'You did tell him I wouldn't want the job, didn't you?'

'Of course I did, darling.' Her mother looked away.

'You told me that Jeremy had suggested me for the job,' Christy pressed. 'Simon on the other hand intimated that it was his idea.'

'He must have already discussed it with Jeremy,' Georgina suggested. 'I promise you I told Jeremy you wouldn't be keen. I couldn't say too much though, darling, not without reminding him what happened six years ago, and I didn't think you'd want that.'

No, her mother was right in that. Jeremy was something of a gossip and she didn't want it put around that she was still suffering from a teenage crush on Simon.

'Well I've agreed to go.' Christy's full mouth compressed when she saw her mother's expression. 'Let's just say he made me an offer I couldn't refuse,' she said with grim humour in answer to her unspoken question. 'A case of rather unsubtle bribery ... besides I've nothing else on.'

Anxiety shadowed her mother's blue eyes. 'Darling are you sure? You aren't doing this simply through bravado are you?'

'Bravely concealing my broken heart you mean?' Christy mocked. 'No Mum, I got over Simon years ago. It's just that my pride still smarts from time to time. As he told me himself at the time all I was really suffering from was infatuation plus lust ... he was, as you aptly said, an extremely sexy man.'

'And still is,' her mother warned her shrewdly, 'possibly more so.'

'Forget it. I'm immune ... innoculated for life. I'd better go down and find out if he intends to stay for lunch. From what he was saying it seems there's some degree of urgency.'

'Umm, he mentioned to Jeremy that his yacht is moored at St Lucia, I expect he'll want to fly out there as soon as he can. Darling, before you go down,' Georgina murmured suddenly, 'can you see if you can find my notes. I suddenly got this idea last night ...'

They had fallen off the bedside table and it took Christy five minutes to uncover them. Leaving her mother to mull over her new 'idea' she went back downstairs, wondering a little wryly just what she had committed herself to. There was no going back now. Simon had played cleverly on her emotions, she had to grant him that, but she wasn't eighteen any longer. She shrugged mentally. All right, she was annoyed at the way he had manoeuvred her, but it had happened and now her best course was simply to treat him as she might Miles or her mother. He was simply another writer for whom she was going to work; someone who was giving her an opportunity to see a part of the world she had always longed to see. He no longer had the power to hurt or humiliate her. That was over and done with.

CHAPTER THREE

THEY flew out to St Lucia three days later. His ketch, *Stormsurf* was moored there in Castries harbour, Simon informed Christy laconically and they would sail from there to the tiny island of St Paul's on which he was based.

Mentally blessing the fact that she had kept the clothes she had used for India the summer before, Christy spent a hectic morning going through them, packing those she thought might be useful.

'Swimsuits, shorts, jeans, that sort of thing,' Simon had told her in reply to her query as to what she would need. 'Don't bother about any diving gear, we'll get you fixed up with that there—saves air-freighting it out and waiting for it.'

Now they were West Indies bound, Simon immersed in some papers he had brought on board with him, and she still did not have a much clearer idea of exactly what they were going to be doing. He wanted to find a sunken wreck he had told her, giving her some brief background details about the man he intended to make the main character of his new book. There hadn't been time for her to do any reading up herself, and wishing she had had the forethought to buy some magazines at the airport, she lay back in her seat and tried to relax. Flying had never been something she enjoyed, although it was the take-offs and landings she really loathed.

'Sorry about this . . .' Simon raised his head from the papers he was studying to smile at her. Christy had already noticed the covert glances their stewardess had given him; hardly surprising really. He must easily be the most attractive man on board. The tawny eyes narrowed suddenly, and Christy wondered if he had picked up on her thoughts. Hardly, she derided herself, he was a man, not a mind-reader. The trouble was, although she was loathe to admit it, she hadn't shaken off entirely the old teenage worshipful awe of him. Oh, consciously she had, of course she had, but her old emotions occasionally sneaked up on her, surprising her, shaking the foundations of self-confidence she had built up so painstakingly. All the more reason to be on her guard, she told herself, acknowledging his apology with a cool smile.

'Jeremy dumped these on me at the last minute.' He picked up the folder and grimaced faintly. 'Tour details from Dee Harland . . . Jeremy knows I prefer to go through them myself. Oh, Dee is the publicity agent Jeremy uses in the States . . .' he added by way of explanation.

His laconic assumption of her ignorance infuriated Christy. 'You don't need to explain who Dee is to me, Simon,' she told him sweetly. 'Actually Dee and I have met.'

She watched the faint narrowing of his eyes, and thought sardonically that she doubted that the relationship he had had with the glamorous American P.R. woman, had been anything like as cool as hers. 'I haven't spent the last six years pining away in the country, Simon,' she added. 'Dee and I met the last time my mother was in the States. I went with her.'

It had been one of his more cruel taunts that she was nothing but a child who had seen and done nothing, and she felt a brief stab of satisfaction in underlining the fact that she was no longer that child. In point of fact although she had enjoyed the experience of her mother's American publicity tour, she did prefer the calm of the English countryside, but there were other ways of broadening one's mind apart from travel. Reading for instance . . . All second-hand knowledge, she taunted herself. What had she really discovered or learned by her own experience?

What she had learned from Simon had been enough, she defended herself mentally. Was it really a crime to be without any ambition other than to live peaceably and content? Hers was a spirit that desired quietude; she found no pleasure in adrenalin-pumping excitement, in confrontation or competition; she never had. Perhaps it was arrogant to feel satisfied with the standards and goals she set for herself, instead of being concerned with meeting those set by others . . . perhaps after her experience with Simon she had deliberately opted out.

'What deep thoughts are you thinking, I wonder?' Simon's voice checked her.

'I was just wondering what we'd get for lunch,' she returned blandly, meeting his eyes.

'Never.' She could see a hint of laughter in them, and something else; a sharp alertness that warned her that he suspected her of deception and would enjoy accusing her of it, simply for the challenge. 'Your eyes never glow such a deep amethyst for anything as mundane as food.'

He was too astute; saw and knew too much. She

must not forget that he was a writer, his mind attuned to the emotional nuances of others.

'Perhaps not at eighteen,' she agreed lightly.

'You're very anxious to persuade me how much you've changed.'

Christy held her breath for a few seconds. This was getting dangerous. 'Am I?' She made a pretence of studying his jibe and then said judiciously, 'I don't think so. *You're* the one who keeps making comparisons.'

He said nothing but his smile made prickles of alarm race across her skin, and she was glad when he changed the subject, talking about India and asking her for her impressions of it.

For the next hour they talked amicably. Simon was a skilled conversationalist, neither hogging the conversation nor letting it drag. Christy had absorbed a good deal during her weeks in India. Working alongside Miles and helping with his research had been something of a challenge initially, but she had loved every minute of it. History had always been one of her favourite subjects, and at one time she had considered taking her degree in it, but the fields open to students with history degrees were very limited and she had concentrated instead on her art.

Listening to him she had to suppress the temptation to sketch Simon. His features were so strong; his bone structure so positive that drawing him was always a visual pleasure. She had sketched him in the past, of course—but all those sketches, drawn with adoration and love, had been destroyed after he had left her. Now her trained eye detected the small differences in him she had noticed on their first meeting, and she studied him covertly.

He seemed to have lost a little of the restlessness which had once been such an integral part of him. She remembered that that summer there had not been a day when he had not taken her somewhere; wanted to do something. He had rarely been content to simply sit and watch. Unlike her he had always been a keen participator in life, never an onlooker. His face had hardened slightly, too; the cynicism in his eyes more noticeable. He was a man it would always be easy for her sex to love, Christy thought perceptively, and yet very hard to know. She knew very little about his background. Six years ago she had been content simply to adore ... she asked for nothing ... questioned nothing.

'Tell me a bit more about what you're doing,' she asked him during a lull in their conversation. 'I know you want to investigate this supposed pirate adventurer with a view to writing about him ...'

'Umm ... the idea came to me last year while I was holidaying with friends on St Paul's—they'd hired a house there—a colonial mansion incorporating the shell of what had apparently once been the home of this Kit Masterson. I was curious ...' He shrugged. 'I asked the locals questions and got to hear the island legend about him.' He paused maddeningly and Christy prodded,

'Well go on, tell me.'

'I only know the basic outline. It seems this Kit Masterson sailed originally with Drake—he must have been little more than a boy. The local rumour is that he'd stowed away on his first voyage. Eventually with Elizabeth's favour he became one of the many English captains harrying the Spanish. No doubt he used the money he amassed sailing with Drake to buy his own ship—a fairly ordinary tale for the times, but it does get more interesting.

'Apparently from one Spanish galleon he took not only the gold but a girl who was being sent from Spain by her family to marry the son of the Governor of one of the Spanish settlements. Initially he tried to ransom her but the Governor refused to accept as a bride for his only son a woman who had been abducted by the English, claiming that her virtue could no longer be guaranteed. By the same token the girl's parents refused to ransom her back—they had other daughters to find husbands for perhaps, who knows, and so Kit Masterson took her to St Paul's—the West Indies at that time were infested with pirate gangs, Jamaica in particular, St Paul's was small enough, its encircling reef dangerous enough to put most captains off. Kit Masterson built a house here, Isabella bore him a son and they were married. Elizabeth died, James came to the throne; many of the English sea-captains were outlawed. James wanted peace with Spain. Kit Masterson, already a wealthy man, saw what was happening and sailed for London intent on buying himself a pardon. By now he had two daughters as well as a son and enough gold to live out the rest of his life in luxury.

'As I said, St Paul's is surrounded by particularly dangerous reefs with very treacherous currents, but Kit had found a safe channel which could only be used at certain states of the tide. He had instituted a system of lights displayed in the top window of his house which he used as a means of guiding his ship through the reef.

'When he returned from London with his pardon, no lights showed from the house; it was a dark night and it was the season for storms. Despite all his skill his ship foundered on the reef, but Kit himself managed to swim free. However, when he reached the house it had been ransacked, his wife and daughters brutally murdered. He discovered later that there had been a pirate raid on the island when he was gone.

'His son had managed to escape, being mistaken for one of his servants and was able to tell his father what had happened. The pirates had been after the gold they were sure he had secreted in the house. The story is that he was so grief stricken by what had happened that he removed all his gold from its hiding places and rowed it out himself to the spot where his ship had gone down, sinking it there . . .'

'And you think it might still be there?'

Simon laughed. 'Hardly . . . Over the years the exact location of the ship has been lost—the tidal wave that struck Kingston in the seventeenth century no doubt reached as far as St Paul's and probably moved the wreck if it actually existed, and as for the gold—I suspect that's just an embellishment added over the years—I doubt very much that a man as hard-headed as Kit Masterson would have had to be had he existed, would have given in to such an emotional impulse. No, the gold, if there was any, is long gone. What I want to discover though, is how much truth, if any, there is in the story, and discovery of the wreck, while not confirming it completely, would go a long way to making it seem possible rather than improbable. My novel will cover the lifetime of Kit; and those of his son and grandson—they were three men who would have lived in the West Indies when they played an extremely important role in the economy of the world—sugar; slaves; the sheer stubborn determination it took to be a European in the West Indies.'

'Surely there are records?'

'Not on St Paul's—if the Masterson family actually existed, don't forget they would have ruled the island as their own kingdom. It did once produce sugar, but getting information out of the locals isn't very easy. Don't forget we're talking about a corner of the world notorious for its superstition and ignorance.'

'Voodoo?' Christy enquired. 'But they don't surely . . .'

'I wouldn't like to say,' Simon checked her, 'perhaps not on the more tourist orientated islands, but it's still a very volatile part of the world. However, at the moment I'm more concerned with the past than the present. I've already checked through the records in London—Elizabeth's ministers were painstaking in their records, but the only small nugget I managed to glean was an entry relating to "the pearl necklace which was given to Her Majesty by the captain of the Golden Fleece". The *Golden Fleece* was the name of Kit Masterson's ship—or so I'm told, but since the Elizabethan records don't mention him by name I can't be sure that he actually did exist.'

'But who owns the house now?' Christy questioned him, feeling the faint beginnings of excitement stir inside her; her imagination had been captured by what he had told her and she was as eager as a small child to know more.

There was a brief silence, and then Simon told her, almost reluctantly it seemed to her. 'I do.'

She felt a momentary start of surprise. Six years ago he had told her quite vehemently that the idea of a permanent settled base, of owning a home and all that it entailed, was an anathema to him. Now it seemed he had changed his mind. She shrugged aside a small dart of pain. Why should she care what he did? Everyone changed with time; hadn't she done so herself?

As the silence grew Christy felt almost as though he expected her to make some comment, but what could she say? To say anything at all would be to admit to him how much she remembered of what he had once said. It was foolish to feel that he was almost disappointed when she didn't comment, but when she asked him if there were any records appertaining to the house he answered her easily enough.

'Some yes, but as I said earlier, the original house was destroyed—probably by a hurricane—and the one that was built on the same site was erected in eighteen eighty by an English cavalryman who had served with Wellington and who bought the island from the Crown because his doctors had advised that to benefit his health he should live somewhere with a hot climate. He was injured in battle apparently, and the island remained in the hands of that family until the time of the Boer War, when both sons were killed. One of the daughters married the son of an English industrialist but by that time the island was no longer a source of wealth. More recently there had been plans to try and develop it as a tourist base complete with marina but the problem of the surrounding reef still remains, so that is now in abeyance.'

It was dark when they landed in St Lucia. Christy

went through the immigration formalities almost numb with sleep. She had still not recovered from the shock of waking up to find she had been sleeping with her head on Simon's shoulder, and his casual acceptance of their intimacy had not reassured her. She had dropped off during the film he had told her, when she had questioned why he had not woken her up, and it seemed pointless waking her.

'Now I know what you're like first thing in the morning,' he teased her as they waited for their luggage. 'Quite a cross-patch.'

She wanted to ignore him. She felt tired and irritable, annoyed with herself and with him. 'What's that supposed to mean?' she asked him curtly. 'That you've changed your mind about wanting me as your assistant?'

His eyebrows rose. 'My goodness, you *are* prickly, aren't you? Nice to know you can be human, and that you don't always keep every emotion rigidly under control.'

He made her sound ridiculously inhibited and she longed to have the quick turn of mind to make some clever retort, but her body ached for sleep; her eyes felt gritty, and she herself felt grubby and travel-worn.

She had a quite ridiculous desire to burst into tears when Simon told her that they had to drive all the way across the island, 'and I warn you the roads are none too good.'

He hadn't lied, but at least the bumpiness of their journey in an ancient American car that was their taxi kept her awake, and by the time they eventually reached Castries she was feeling much more alert.

His ketch, he told her, was not moored in the main harbour but in a small marina a mile or so away.

'It's part of a new complex, and I've booked us both into the hotel for tonight—it will take us most of tomorrow to get the stuff we need together, if I know the islanders, and it will give you a chance to get over any jet lag.'

Silently digesting the 'you', Christy wondered wryly how he managed to stay so alert and awake. Perhaps because he was used to the long flight; perhaps because he simply had more endurance. He had always struck her as a tough character; a man who responded to all of life's challenges, and it occurred to her now to wonder what his earlier life had been to give him that hard edge of determination that said he would let nothing stand in the way of his goals.

Stop wondering, she warned herself. You're not going to get involved—remember?

The marina was bordered by a new stretch of road, wide enough to include a parking square. In contrast with Castries it was well lit; strings of gaily coloured lanterns illuminating the jetties. Christy could see the gleam of water between the crush of expensive, white-painted hulls. People, most of them obviously holiday-makers, strolled in the square. On the landward side she could see an arcade of shops which seemed to include a couple of restaurants.

'All this is owned by the hotel,' Simon told her. 'Quite a financial undertaking, but it seems to be paying off.'

One particular group caught Christy's eye. Half a dozen or so people were grouped together under one of the elegant Victorian street lights, most of them male, but it was the girl with them that caught Christy's attention as their taxi stopped. Small, and blonde, she was laughing up at one of her male companions, her face clear beneath the illumination of the lamp. She was as perfect and pretty as a china doll, Christy thought, watching her; her tight white jeans and clinging top revealing a model slim figure, her blonde hair cascading softly on to her shoulders. She was the epitome of what she, Christy, had always secretly wanted to be, and she grimaced ruefully to herself, comparing what she privately considered her almost Amazonian build to the fragility of that possessed by the blonde-haired girl. She had long ago come to terms with her own looks; their gypsy-like wildness no longer made her feel uncomfortable, indeed she was almost able to derive a certain wry amusement from other people's reaction to them. It was a nuisance at times convincing some men that her nature did not match her looks, but she was unable to compress a small pang of envy as she watched the other girl.

Simon got out of the taxi and opened her door for her, paying off their driver and yanking out their bags.

'It's only a few yards from here to the hotel, and I thought you might like to see *Stormsurf* before we go up there.'

He had barely finished speaking when the blonde girl suddenly detached herself from her friends, and called out excitedly, 'Simon!'

She had, Christy noted unworthily, an extremely shrill voice, almost unpleasantly so, but she had no time to formulate any other thoughts because, totally unexpectedly, she was in Simon's arms, her indignant struggles quelled by their hard pressure, his eyes grimly warning as he spun her round so that his back was towards the interested crowd. 'Don't say a word,' he told her. 'Just play along with me, okay?'

She couldn't have spoken even if she had wanted to, for the very good reason that Simon's mouth was covering her own. It had been six years since she had last felt the touch of those firm male lips, and although she had been kissed many times since with varying degrees of skill, she was alarmed to discover that memories were no match for the real thing. She kept her mouth firmly closed, refusing to relax into Simon's embrace, but not fighting him either. Her eyes remained open and she met the fierce glitter of his, wondering if his anger was because she refused to respond or because he had felt the kiss to be necessary.

Why should he *want* her to respond? she asked herself, fighting against the sensations aroused by the pressure of Simon's hand low down on her spine. He was forcing her against his body, his mouth moving over hers with what to any onlooker would seem to be total sensuality.

Perhaps she was wrong to fight him, Christy thought. Perhaps by doing so she was simply showing him that she feared she still might be vulnerable. His muttered, 'Relax, for God's sake and try and look as though you're enjoying it,' reinforced her thoughts. A tiny dart of anger leapt along her nerve endings. Who was he to assume he could use her like a feelingless pawn in whatever game he was now playing? So he wanted to be seen in a passionate clinch with her did he?

Consciously she let her body relax, moving lazily against the hard outline of his, her arms, which had been trapped between them, lifting to close round him, her lips parting as she let her head fall back under the pressure of his kiss.

The small shudder that racked her as the sudden fierce demand of his mouth increased wasn't entirely fabricated. 'Careful,' she warned herself, 'very, very careful.'

'Simon.'

It was the childishly high feminine voice, underlined with jealousy, that brought the kiss to an end, but before he lifted his head, she managed to murmur softly against his mouth, 'I hope that was satisfactory.'

She knew he had heard her. His eyes glittered molten gold over her face before he released her, and turned to the intruder.

'Heavens, she makes me look like Goliath,' was Christy's first thought quickly followed by the knowledge that the childish exterior and manner was simply a pose. Venom flashed bitterly from the blonde's blue eyes as they made a dismissive tour of Christy's face and person.

'Simon, darling, where have you been?'

No attempt to include her in the conversation, Christy noted. She must have a skin like hide. She doubted that she could have intruded so positively on a man who was very plainly with another woman.

'London,' Simon replied easily, adding, 'Mary-Lou, let me introduce you to an old friend of mine, Christy.'

So she had been right in suspecting a faintly American accent Christy thought, noting the girl's forename. Although she suspected they were of a similar age, the disparaging glance with which she dismissed Christy, suggested that out of everything

Simon had said when introducing her, all she had
heard was the adjective 'old'. She was very clever,
Christy thought, wryly admiring her technique, she
had to give her that. She doubted in the same
circumstances if she could have been as positive.

'You missed my birthday party.' A provocative pout
accompanied the words, and Christy had an illuminating vision of that same pout at forty, and then fifty.
Perhaps it was better not to look like a pretty little doll
after all.

'My apologies, but it couldn't be avoided.'

Another pout, plus a sidelong glance through lashes
Christy suspected were never naturally that seductively
dark colour.

'Never mind, you can make it up to me by taking
me out to dinner tomorrow night.'

'Sorry, Mary-Lou, that's impossible. Christy and I
sail for St Paul's tomorrow.'

Now there was no disguising the hostility in her
eyes.

'Really?' A sharply bitter laugh splintered the
silence that suddenly seemed to have fallen. Christy
felt something akin to sympathy for her. Simon was
hardly letting her down lightly, and by now they had
gathered a rather interested audience in the group
Mary-Lou had been with when they arrived.

'How very romantic,' she said brittley to Christy. 'I
do hope you're not sea-sick.'

Watching her flounce angrily back to join her
friends, Christy felt both tired and angry.

Before Simon could speak she said through gritted
teeth. 'The next time you want to get rid of an
unwanted admirer, please don't involve me.' Her eyes

flashed bitterly as she added unwisely. 'You've changed, Simon, you never used to need help in that direction.'

She heard him swear and stepped back automatically. 'I don't know what you're thinking,' he told her curtly, 'but I never have been and never intend to be involved with Mary Lou. Unfortunately, however, she's extremely persistent—when politeness fails other, more draconian measures sometimes have to be used. Her father is one of the major shareholders in the hotel and marina complex, and unfortunately she's grown up under the illusion that the combination of his wealth and her looks is irresistible. She might be in with more of a chance if she wasn't so eager to open her mouth,' he added sardonically, 'and besides,' he looked at Christy and smiled, and she felt the warmth of it curl all the way down to her toes, 'sugary blonde, little-girl prettiness never did a thing for me—you should know that.'

It must be because she was tired that she had to fight so hard against the pull he was exerting over her senses, Christy thought wearily.

'Pity you didn't tell me that before we left,' she came back smartly. 'I could have bought a blonde wig.' The moment the words were out she wished them unsaid, glad of the darkness to hide her angry flush of colour as she realised that she had unwittingly indicated that their relationship could be anything but strictly that of employer and employee, and Simon, damn him, although he was saying nothing, was far too astute to have missed it.

'I doubt that either of us is in the mood to look at *Stormsurf* now,' was all he said. 'You're practically falling asleep on your feet. Let's get up to the hotel and get some sleep.'

CHAPTER FOUR

'LIKE it?' They were down at the marina, standing on one of the piers, looking down at the graceful lines of Simon's ketch. Christy had done some sailing in her teens and knew enough about boats to recognise the power and elegance of this one.

'When I can, I like to use sail, but she has an excellent sea-going engine, which we'll need for some of our work. We can only dive at certain times, and they won't always correspond with favourable winds. Want to have a look round?'

Christy nodded her head, and followed him down the steps on to the gently rolling deck.

Simon took her first through the controls, slowly explaining each one. 'There could be times when you'll have to take control up here, but I'll make sure you get some experience of handling her first. Everything's pretty simple and straightforward.' He turned back towards the companionway and Christy followed him. Below deck the ketch had a surprisingly roomy main salon which Simon explained could double as an extra bedroom.

'We won't need it this trip. She's built to sleep eight with ease. There are two double cabins with a bathroom in between besides the ones we're using and of course the galley. Come and have a look.'

The galley was efficiently equipped; there shouldn't be too many problems preparing food in there, Christy decided, noting the small freezer and the generous storage space.

'This is my cabin.' Simon pushed open a door, and Christy glanced briefly round the small tidy room. 'You could have had your pick, but there's nothing to choose between them, and my stuff was already stored in here.' He closed the door and opened another one, 'Bathroom.'

Once again it was well equipped with a shower as well as a bath.

'And this will be your cabin.' It was an exact replica of his own but on the other side of the ketch. 'There isn't a lock on the door,' he told her drily, 'but we can always get one should you feel it necessary.'

He was deliberately trying to goad her, Christy was sure. Giving him a level look she said calmly. 'Why on earth should I? You're quite safe, Simon,' she added crisply. 'Unlike Mary-Lou, I don't need the message reinforcing, I got it loud and clear the first time round. I know quite well that you don't desire me, and . . .'

She wasn't allowed to get as far as telling him that any lack of desire was mutual because he was staring at her, frowning slightly as he folded his arms and leaned back against the door, effectively cutting off any means of escape. With both of them in it the tiny cabin was almost claustrophobic. He was playing with her, Christy was sure. Why? Had it occurred to him that she might still harbour some remnants of that teenage adoration? Was he intent on making it clear that he felt nothing towards her? If so . . .

'Now where I wonder did you get that idea?' He said it so quietly, and she was so engrossed in her own train of thought that his words took several seconds to penetrate.

'I never said I didn't *desire* you, Christy,' he told her softly. 'I simply said I didn't want to marry you.'

His words came as too much of a shock for her to dissemble. 'But you rejected me,' she reminded him. 'When I came to your room . . .'

'Dear God, Christy, that wasn't *rejection*.' He took hold of her arms and stared down at her. 'How much have you grown up in six years? Not a good deal if you still think that.' He looked grim and angry, and she felt her own anger stir. Why should what had happened so long ago have any relevance now?

'Of course I desired you.' He said it flatly. 'But you made it plain that you wanted marriage. You came to my room prepared to barter your virginity for my wedding ring, and *that* was what I rejected.'

His words were almost a verbal blow even though they were delivered without heat, and humiliatingly, Christy could see that in his eyes her actions must have seemed to be some sort of trade off. She had wanted him to marry her, of course; had hoped that once he had made love to her he would want to marry her; but she had never intended using her virginity as a lever. She opened her mouth to tell him as much and then changed her mind. What was the point?

'Where will you store the diving equipment?' she asked instead.

Simon let her change the subject without comment, showing her the storage areas in the main salon.

'There's an excellent place just off the marina where they stock all the latest stuff. Scuba and deep-sea diving are all the rage here at the moment, so we won't have any trouble getting everything we need.' He glanced at his watch.

'In fact we'd better get over there now. It's a four-hour sail to St Paul's and I'd like to be there before dusk.

'St Paul's is a very small island, and the intensity of the currents off the reef are dependent to some extent on the winds. Any day now they should start to change, and once they do that will be our only chance to dive, so I want to be ready.'

'And the rest of the time?'

He shrugged. 'I've done some notes, I'd like them typing up . . . You could talk to Pierre the gardener—he's the one I learned the legend from originally . . . I wouldn't mind some sketches of how you think the original house might have looked . . . Perhaps even a few rough sketches of how you imagine Kit and Isabella . . . I always find it helps me to have something concrete to look at when I'm writing. Obviously we're not going to be able to find out what either of them looked like but Jeremy told me that the powerfully vivid verbal portraits Miles was able to draw of his main characters was thanks to you.'

It was true that she had done several sketches for Miles of the main characters in his Indian novel, but then she had had some guidelines to work on. Ridiculously, when she tried to visualise Kit all she could see was an Elizabethan-clad image of Simon, which was illogical, Kit would probably have been fair . . . his hair bleached even fairer by the sun and the salt . . . his skin would have been tanned, of course . . . Images began to take shape in her imagination and her fingers itched for a pencil.

'You mean you'd actually trust my judgment to that extent?'

Simon shrugged. 'Why shouldn't I? You've already proved your ability, and if I don't agree with what you produce I can always tell you.'

Harsh sunlight hit Christy's eyes as they went back on deck, she put on her glasses and followed Simon back on to dry land, letting him grasp her hand, to pull her on to the jetty beside him. Her hand looked surprisingly slim and vulnerable, encased in the masculinity of his. She saw that he was looking at her, and wished a little uncomfortably that her shorts were less brief. They were old ones—shorts hadn't been something she needed in India, and it had been so long since she had been away on a seaside holiday that most of her beach-type clothes were relics from her schooldays. Her shorts were denim and very old, but they were comfortable and sensible for clambering about a boat on. Mentally comparing her appearance with the delicately feminine one of Mary-Lou, Christy suppressed a shrug. What did it matter what she wore, she was here to work, not to act as an ornament.

'Finished?' she enquired sweetly as Simon lifted his eyes from his lazy inspection of her legs.

'Just about.' He grinned without any trace of embarrassment. 'I'd forgotten just how long they were. Almost as long as mine.' He said it softly, and Christy was powerless to prevent her sudden surge of colour as her mind dredged up an unexpectedly intimate picture of the two of them; their bodies entwined, Simon's powerful thighs imprisoning hers. It had been one of those afternoons on the beach she remembered and her stomach quivered protestingly.

To punish herself for allowing the memory to surface, and angry with Simon for deliberately encouraging it to do so, by injecting an unwarranted intimacy into their conversation, she said disinterestedly, 'Were they? I can't remember.' The jetty was narrow and they were standing almost breast to breast. Wicked lights danced in Simon's eyes as he leaned towards her, and murmured, 'Want me to prove it?'

Her heart was thudding crazily but she managed to retort sedately, 'I'll take your word for it.' She walked away from him, intent on escaping the powerfully hypnotic spell his proximity seemed to place on her, but as she did so, she thought she heard him saying teasingly, 'Pity.'

She must not read anything more than a basic male instinct into his manner, she warned herself as they walked through the marina. If Simon suddenly seemed sexually interested in her it could only be out of boredom or because she represented a challenge, while she would be in danger of . . .

Of what? she asked herself, suddenly chilled. Of nothing surely? She was immune to Simon, wasn't she? Tiny tremors of sensation coursed through her body. Of course she was immune; it was ridiculous to imagine anything else; the tense inner excitement she was experiencing was caused purely by her interest in Kit's story—nothing else.

Firmly suppressing her thoughts she followed Simon towards the entrance to the marine store. She was here to do a job that was all. To do a job and exorcise a ghost. The ghost of her love for Simon.

They spent close on three hours in the shop. Simon

was extremely meticulous over the purchase of Christy's diving equipment. Although the water would be warm she would need a wet suit to protect her skin from cuts and grazes. 'Remember, we're talking about diving down to a coral reef,' he told her, 'and coral grazes can be extremely dangerous.' The diving gear, although American, operated in a way that was familiar to her. It was some time since she had last dived but everything she had been taught came flooding back to her, and when eventually they left she was in an excited, happy frame of mind.

They went back to the hotel to collect their luggage, and after a light meal returned to the marina. As he had promised the shop owner had had their purchases delivered to the *Stormsurf* and Christy checked over them while Simon went ashore to collect provisions.

'We'll take mainly dried and frozen stuff,' he told her. 'I don't envisage us having to stay on board for anything other than brief periods—two or three nights at the most. We'll be based on St Paul's and will only need to remain at sea if we find anything interesting.'

He returned just as Christy finished her task, and for several minutes they worked efficiently together stowing away his purchases.

'This feels heavy.' He handed her a small case.

'My portable typewriter, I wasn't sure if you had one. It's always handy to have.'

'Mmm. There's a full-sized one at the house—not electric I'm afraid, the generator that supplies us with power is rather temperamental so I opted for a manual. Are we ready to cast off?'

Nodding her agreement Christy went up on deck to

help him, standing at the side as she watched the harbour slide gently away.

As Simon had said, the ketch could be sailed single-handed. Today to save time he was using the engine and invited Christy to join him and take her turn at the wheel. When she had proved to his satisfaction that she could handle it he showed her some charts. 'This one is of the seas round St Paul's. You can see how deep the water outside the reef is. My guess is that St Paul's was once a larger island which has partially submerged. These islands are volcanic and subject to structural change. In Kit Masterson's time there was obviously only one safe way into the lagoon. Now there are several—natural fissures created by volcanic movement no doubt, but it does make it harder for us to pin down the exact spot where his ship is likely to have gone down. What makes it harder still is that the original house was destroyed. As you'll see when we get there, the house is built on a projecting spit of land and so looks out to sea on three sides. From studying wind and current charts, my guess is that his channel was probably somewhere around here.' Simon drew a pencil ring on the chart. 'Unfortunately, that's also the place where the currents are strongest.' He put down his pencil and frowned. 'When we do dive it will always be attached to a line and I don't want you staying down for longer than an hour at a time at the most.'

'The tanks hold enough air for two hours plus twenty minutes emergency supply.'

'I know, but I don't intend to take any chances. One hour will be our maximum.'

'Have you thought about aerial photography?'

Christy asked him. 'Several wrecks have been located using it.'

'It did occur to me but if she's there I suspect the *Golden Fleece* has broken up and is now covered in coral. I don't think there'll be enough of her left to show up on a photograph.'

A pleasant breeze was blowing, its buffet invigorating. She had forgotten the pleasure of being at sea, Christy reflected although Simon's ketch was far more luxurious than the dinghies she had sailed in as a teenager.

'A bit different from the Channel,' she commented to him, throwing her head back so that the wind could lift her hair and cool her scalp. 'Where did you learn to sail?' She had never questioned about his past; he had simply arrived in her life and dominated it. What did she really know about him, Christy mused. The blurb on his book jackets gave away very little about him, and she could never recall him talking about his family or childhood.

'I was taught by an extremely dour Scotsman.'

She waited for him to continue. 'Unlike you I did not have an enchanted childhood, Christy. I was illegitimate and my mother abandoned me. I was adopted but it didn't work out. The couple who adopted me had a child of their own a couple of years later, and rightly or wrongly I always felt second-best. I ran away when I was twelve and ended up in front of the juvenile court for pinching fruit from a barrow— luckily for me. I'd only been in London a couple of days—living rough as hundreds of kids do every year. The Judge counselled that I was to spend a month at a special rehabilitation centre in Scotland. It was run by a Liverpudlian couple—he was ex-army, a disciplinarian with the proverbial heart of gold. I suppose I can best describe the place as a sort of an outward bound course for would-be juvenile delinquents. It taught me a lot—about myself as well as about others. By the time the month was up I could understand why I had felt the need to rebel. The same Scotsman who taught me to sail also told me that education was the golden key that unlocked all doors. At first I didn't believe him—I was a tough little cynic, convinced that I knew it all, but he had made me wonder . . . I went back home, worked harder at school, found that I enjoyed channelling my energies and using them. Eventually I got a scholarship to Oxford. When I left I tried my hand at several things; roamed round the world a bit. I worked in a winery in California . . . a cattle station in Australia. I went to South Africa, India and came back not really knowing what I wanted to do. I met Jeremy at a cocktail party in London and it was something he said that made me wonder if I could write.'

'And your . . . parents?' Christy probed gently. She was stunned by what he had told her; and the cool manner in which he had related it as though he were talking about someone else. Was that careless indifference a shield he used to protect himself from pain, she wondered perceptively.

'We meet occasionally. All my teenage bitterness is gone now. They did their best by me and with hindsight I can see that even had I been brought up by my natural parents things might have turned out the same. I was always rebellious . . . restless . . .'

'And . . . and your real mother?'

His eyebrows rose.

'Have you ever thought of trying to trace her?' Christy asked when it was obvious that he wasn't going to help her. How crassly curious she felt, and how much she wished the question unvoiced.

'Not in the last ten years. Once perhaps yes, but I've long since come to believe that we are what we make ourselves. To search for an unknown mother in the belief that finding her would put right whatever deficiencies there might be in my life seems childish. She was only young—I know that from my adoptive parents. No doubt she's made a fresh life for herself— I certainly hope so. We'd be meeting as strangers, each feeling compelled to feel an emotion for the other we might not necessarily be able to feel. The day I finally stopped thinking that if I found my mother, it would solve all my problems, I knew I was adult,' he told her with a wry grimace.

While she could see the sense of what he was saying, Christy could also see now why he was so restless, so reluctant to commit himself to a permanent relationship; so determined to be free of emotional bondage.

'Look.' His command distracted her, and she focused on the horizon. 'There's St Paul's now.'

It was no more than a faint blur, but as she watched it gew larger until she could actually make out wooded slopes and a steep hill rising above them.

'Although it's much smaller in many ways it's very similar to St Lucia,' Simon told her. 'If you look to your left, you should soon be able to make out the promontory and the house.'

By straining her eyes she was just able to do so, and

a tiny thrill of excitement seized her. The island looked so tranquil, floating on the dense blue of the Caribbean; was this how Kit Masterson had felt the first time he saw it? A peaceful island haven? Suddenly she itched for her sketch pad, images crowding into her mind. Dashing down to her cabin she snatched it up, racing back topside, sketching furiously as the island drew nearer. Simon said nothing, concentrating on sailing the ketch, and for once Christy was barely conscious of him.

Under her gifted fingers images took shape on her pad; a small, sturdy English vessel, built for speed and agility, its captain standing on deck, watching as his men let down the lead-weighted line to check the depth of the channel. Christy drew him bare-headed, lean and muscular, calling on her knowledge of the Elizabethan period to give him that same clever, educated intelligence she had seen in so many of Nicholas Hilliard's miniatures. The Elizabethans had been men of letters and guile, skilled with the tongue as well as the sword. Would Isabella have loved him? Surely, yes ... He would have been vastly different from the rigidly correct Spaniards she must have known; and she was his captive ... had she known then, watching the island take shape as she herself was doing, what was to be her fate? That she was to be his wife; bear his children ... and then die for the sake of his gold, Christy reminded herself with a sudden chill shiver.

Not wanting to draw any more she closed her sketchbook and put down her pencil. For a moment then the past had been too real.

They were in a small natural harbour with a rickety

wooden jetty, and Simon was already dropping anchor.

'They'll have seen us from the house and will send someone down for our stuff,' he told her. 'The roads are so bad the only form of transport worth using is a Land-Rover, but the beaches are superb.'

'Are there many privately owned villages?' Christy asked him. He had mentioned once that the island was as yet undeveloped, and she sensed that he preferred it that way.

'Half a dozen or so, and there's only one coastal town if you can call it that, and another inland village. The town's in the next but one bay, the island's main source of income comes from bananas, you'll see them growing further inland.' He stopped speaking and glanced along the dusty track leading from the beach. Listening, Christy heard the unmistakable sound of an engine.

'Here comes our transport.'

It was the oldest Land-Rover Christy had ever seen, driven by a beaming teenager, dressed in bright red cut-off shorts.

'Pierre's grandson, Georges,' Simon told her. 'Come and meet him.'

It didn't take them long to get their things stacked in the back of the Land-Rover. It possessed only one bench seat and Christy found herself wedged between Simon and the door.

'Hang on a minute,' he told her, turning slightly and lifting his arm, curving it round her. 'That gives us a little more room.'

Christy was uncomfortably aware of the maleness of Simon's body. What's the matter with you? she chided herself, relax for heaven's sake. She was relieved when their drive turned out to be a very brief one, her discomfort forgotten as she stared in delight at the house.

It was a colonial mansion in miniature, passion flowers rambling over its lower storey. Bright blue shutters flanked the windows, colourful shrubs broke up the impossible green of the lawn.

'Come on we're here,' Simon told her unnecessarily, removing his arm. She felt curiously bereft without it, almost stumbling out into the heat.

'Leave your things, we'll get those later,' Simon commanded. 'Let's go inside.'

Inside a fan whirred soporifically from the ceiling, dispersing the heavy heat of the afternoon, white walls and a polished floor gleamed immaculately in the empty hallway.

'In here.' Simon opened a door and pushed her gently inside. Here the walls were a delicate pale green, the floor once again polished and covered by several off-white rugs. The furniture was cane and painted a slightly deeper shade of green than the walls. A delicately striped fabric covered the cushions and hung at the windows.

'I bought it furnished,' Simon told her laconically. 'The previous owner had bought it for his second wife. When he divorced her to marry his third, she refused to set foot in it.' He moved to the door and opened it calling out, 'Helen, how about some tea?'

Ten minutes later Christy heard footsteps outside and the rattle of a trolley.

'Helen is Georges' mother and Pierre's daughter,' Simon informed her. 'She's a widow, and between them the three of them, they run the house.'

The woman who came in was fat by European standards, her print dress straining across her ample body as she beamed at them.

'Well, well, this be the lady who's going to help you find that old wreck then?'

'The same,' Simon said with a smile, 'Christy, come and meet Helen.'

Shrewd black eyes studied her and Christy felt as though she were undergoing some sort of test. She must have passed because Helen beamed at her. 'I can see you and me's going to get along just fine,' she told Christy in her sing-song English. 'If you like I'll show you up to your room.'

'Yes, you go with her,' Simon told her, 'but don't be too long, otherwise your tea will go cold.'

She followed Helen up two flights of stairs to a galleried landing. 'This here be the top floor,' Helen told her, wheezing slightly, 'and Mr Simon he said you were to have this room especially.' She stopped and opened a door, and Christy followed her inside, gasping with pleasure as she saw the view from her window. She could see right over the promontory and into the distance, the sea so incredibly blue that it looked almost unreal. The bedroom was decorated in delicate grey and white and had she saw, its own *en suite* bathroom.

'Miss Anabelle, she had all new bathrooms put in when she was mistress here,' Helen told her proudly. 'Finest house on the island this be.'

'The room's lovely,' Christy told her. Everything was crisply clean, the bedlinen starched and white, and as for the view ... Long after Helen had gone Christy stood there, too entranced by it to move away.

At last she forced herself to go downstairs. Simon was sitting in a chair drinking a cup of tea. She thanked him for his forethought in selecting her room, knowing she sounded stilted and irritated with herself for doing so.

'I thought it would appeal to you,' was all he said.

'You mean all that virgin white?' Christy asked tartly, wishing she hadn't when she saw the look on his face.

'Hardly applicable now, surely Christy? Actually when I chose it for you I was thinking of the view,' he added with mild irony, 'nothing else.

'If you feel up to it when you've had your tea, I'd like you to come to my study—it's across the hall. I want to show you my filing system and go through the way I do my notes.'

He didn't stay, leaving her alone to drink her tea, her eyes drawn to his tall, jean-clad body as he walked out of the room.

Christy didn't rush her tea, and it was a good fifteen minutes before she followed him. She found him sitting behind a desk, sorting through some papers. It didn't take long for him to explain to her his systems; they were quite straightforward, his method of collating his notes far more organised than that used by either Miles or her mother.

'Come over here for a minute,' he commanded her when he had finished. He walked over to the window and Christy followed him, noticing as she did so the telescope standing in front of it.

'Stand here and look through this,' he instructed her.

He was standing right behind her, leaning over her,

and she could feel the heat coming off his body, the weight of his hand on her shoulder. 'Now if you look straight ahead you should be able to see the reef . . . just to the left of it is the spot where I think Kit's ship went down . . . Got it?'

She had found the reef, sharp, dragon's teeth of dangerous coral ready to tear out the bottom of any unwary craft. 'Yes . . . yes . . . I think I've got it,' she told him, watching the boil of angry water surging against the channel that must lead into the lagoon. Despite the intense blue of the sea there was something quite definitely menacing and dangerous about the reef and the boiling sea and she shivered a little, tensing as Simon's hand moved, examining the exposed flesh of her shoulder.

'Cold?' he queried sharply

'No, just good old-fashioned fear,' Christy told him. 'That reef looks dangerous.'

'Not just looks. It is. Tomorrow, if you're feeling up to it, we'll take a boat out to it—not the ketch, but a motor boat we use inside the lagoon and you can get a closer look. By the way another warning, if you fancy going swimming. Watch out for sharks. They come inside the reef sometimes.'

Sharks. Christy shivered. Of course there would be sharks in these waters.

'Don't worry, they won't bother you if you keep well away,' Simon reassured her, sensing her tension. He was still standing behind her, his hand resting on her nape and she could feel a dangerous temptation to lean back against him. They both moved at the same time, Christy shuddering as she felt the warm persuasion of his mouth moving against the side of her throat, his fingers pushing aside the straps of her top and bra, to stroke her smooth flesh.

'Simon, don't . . .'

He was just about to turn her in his arms when Helen walked in, and instead he released her. Moving away from him on legs that were decidedly shaky, Christy waited until Helen had asked him what time he wanted her to serve their evening meal, and left them, to say tensely, 'Simon, let's get one thing straight. I came here to work for you—nothing more, and work is all I want to do.'

'Meaning that although you might have been prepared to share Miles' bed, you don't have a similar desire to share mine.' He smiled at her and despite his relaxed pose, she had the distinct impression that in reality he was both tense and angry. 'Very well, but if you should change your mind.'

'I won't.' She snapped the words out at him; angry that he should think her capable of sharing a man's bed so lightly. 'If you don't mind, I think I'll go up and have a shower.' She stepped past him warily, not looking at him as she hurried towards the door. She was beginning to wonder if after all she had done the right thing in coming here with him. When she had agreed, she had not realised that sexually he found her desirable. That knowledge disturbed her—not because she found it offensive—on the contrary she found it dangerously exciting and it was *that* that disturbed her.

CHAPTER FIVE

'ARE you okay?'

They were in a small motor boat heading out over the lagoon to the spot Simon had shown her through the telescope the previous day.

'Fine.' Christy managed to make herself heard above the raucous sound of the small engine, gazing appreciatively at her surroundings. Even close to, the sea was impossibly turquoise and so clear here that she could see to the bottom. Inside the lagoon the water was relatively calm, a constant temptation to any swimmer. Twisting round she looked back in the direction they had come. Steep stone steps led down the cliff from the house to an almost perfect crescent-shaped beach covered in soft pale sand. They were right at the end of the promontory, and beyond the lagoon she could see where the opposing currents of the Atlantic and the Caribbean fought for supremacy. The day was so clear she could see the distant blur of other islands much further away than they seemed, so Simon had told her. Already she could feel the heat of the sun burning through her thin cotton shirt, and was thankful that she had taken the time to put some sun-block on her face. Normally she didn't burn but she had no wish to end up looking like a dried prune. She had woken up this morning totally disorientated for several minutes, unused to sleeping so deeply. When she had remembered where she was she had been appalled to discover that it was gone ten o'clock, and to find that there was a cold cup of tea beside her bed. Simon had brought her to work—not to sleep. Even so, despite her rush to get downstairs and apologise for her tardiness she had lingered long enough to stare out of her window and wonder if perhaps it had been on this spot that Isabella had stood to watch for her adventuring husband.

Simon had soon reassured her that her lateness had not interfered with his plans. 'I thought it best to let you catch up on your sleep,' he told her lazily, coming out from behind his desk, where he had been studying some papers. 'You were absolutely dead to the world when I came in with your tea.'

So it had been Simon and not Helen who had brought the tea. The thought of Simon standing over her, perhaps watching her, brought her out in a rash of goosebumps.

Unwilling to analyse her reactions too deeply Christy dragged her thoughts forward. Like her, Simon was dressed casually in faded denim shorts and a thin shirt, but unlike her he had his shirt unfastened almost to the waist, revealing the hard muscles of his chest and the dark feathering of body hair that disappeared beneath the waistband of his shorts. Both of them were wearing shoes—a necessary precaution Simon had told her, just in case for any reason they had to get out and walk over the coral, but unlike her Simon did not seem to need sunglasses, his eyes screwing up slightly as he steered the boat towards the reef.

Through the telescope Christy had felt something of its menace but not all of it. Close to, it threw shadows that chilled the water of the lagoon, sharp, ragged spears breaking through the foam to warn of what lurked below.

The channel Simon had pointed out to her was fairly wide; and it was at this point that the lagoon was deepest he told her, something which would have been in its favour for Kit Masterson's purposes. 'He would have needed a reasonable draft for his ship, but if, as I suspect the coral walls form a sharply v-shaped channel, it would have needed a considerable amount of skill to negotiate them.'

They had not brought their diving suits but now that she had seen the site where Simon proposed they begin looking she could understand why he had stipulated dives of no longer than an hour at a time. It was easy to lose all sense of time underwater; and these waters would be particularly dangerous. The Caribbean was a graveyard of ships and many divers had lost their lives searching for the wreckage of them.

Out beyond the reef some activity caught her eye and she froze as she saw the sharp fins cutting through the waves.

'Don't worry. They shouldn't bother us too much when we start diving,' Simon told her. 'The water's too rough for them to want to bask in it. I've been checking through the weather reports this morning, and with a bit of luck we should be able to start diving the day after tomorrow.'

Christy had seen the reports on his desk, and he had shown her the radio he used to monitor all the local weather broadcasts. This information together with all the data he had collected of the weather patterns during previous summers had enabled him to pinpoint a time when the currents were least likely to be affected by the winds.

'We'll go back now,' he told her, turning the boat neatly. 'Now that you've seen the reef close to you'll realise what we're up against. It isn't going to be like diving off the side of the local swimming baths,' he added warningly. 'In fact I intend to do most of the diving myself with you acting as a back up. If we weren't so short of time I'd do it all.'

It didn't take too long to get back to the beach, but to Christy's surprise once they did, instead of heading back to the house, Simon suggested that they stay on the beach for a while.

'I'm still suffering a little from the effects of jet lag myself,' he told her with a brief smile. 'Once we start working we won't get many opportunities to relax. Georges should have brought our lunch down, I asked Helen if he would before we left.'

He had done. It was in a huge wicker picnic basket under the shade of a beach umbrella that he must have brought down as well, and there were also a couple of large beach towels.

'Fancy a swim?' Simon asked her. 'Or would you prefer to eat?'

'After that huge breakfast,' Christy laughed protestingly, 'I'd love a swim.'

Luckily she had put her bikini on under her shorts and top, and it didn't take her more than a minute to strip them off. She had expected Simon to go into the water ahead of her, but when she emerged from her shirt, she found he was standing a bare metre away, studying her with an entirely male appreciation that sent flickers of awareness darting over her body. Stop it, she warned herself. You've been down that road once and you don't like where it leads. By telling her that he still desired her, Simon had put the onus of keeping their relationship platonic and businesslike on her shoulders, and she was determined to show him that she was completely impervious to him, and treat him as she would any other male she barely knew who had made the same statement. The trouble was that Simon wasn't merely any other male; he was a devastatingly sexy one whose mere presence played havoc with her pulse rate and who exerted a magnetic pull over her senses that she wanted to respond to with an alarming intensity every time she saw him. Of course she didn't still love him; how could she, but she couldn't deny that she did still find him attractive. He had been the first man to awaken her after all; the first man she had loved. The *only* man she had loved, she reminded herself grimly. She had already made one bad mistake in thinking herself completely immune to him; it would be madness to make another in underestimating the danger of his sexual attraction by telling herself she was safe because she no longer loved him.

Strangely enough the one emotion she did not feel towards him was hatred. She had expected to but that particular emotion had just not been there. In a matter of a couple of days she had learned far more about him than she had in a whole summer, but of course now they met as equal adults and not adolescent and adult and although as a writer she admired him, she was no longer a worshipping acolyte content merely to be allowed to adore.

'Well, are we going to swim?'

She had been so engrossed in her thoughts that for a

second she looked at him blankly. He had taken off his shirt, but retained his faded denims, and unknowingly she must have been studying them because he said softly, 'Normally I wouldn't bother, but something tells me that all grown up and adult though you are, you might.'

He was telling her that normally he swam in the nude; well why not, this part of the lagoon was, after all, completely private. Strangely enough his comment brought not shock, but a wave of intense excitement. In her mind's eye she could see him, his body strong but supple; man completely at one with the elements. Pushing aside her mental image of his body tanned and sleek, she ran into the lagoon, not waiting to see if Simon was following before launching into a speedy crawl. She had always been a good swimmer, but she had forgotten the special pleasure of feeling her body move through the water. She dived, briefly touching the bottom, watching the scatter of small gaily coloured fish and then coming up slowly testing her breath control, and treading water. Simon was nowhere in sight. Some sixth sense made her glance down, the dark shadow of his body as he swam swiftly underwater towards her almost menacing in its speed. She waited until the last minute to avoid him, diving down and then surfacing quickly and for half an hour they indulged in an energetic game of chase. In speed and strength Simon could easily outstrip her but Christy thought her deftness and agility gave her an edge over him until he out-manoeuvred her, gripping her firmly with his legs and forcing her to sink down to the sea bed with him, his arms imprisoning her before he let them float slowly to the surface. Once there, Christy broke free and headed for the beach. There had been something so openly sensual about the way he had held her, that her instincts warned her that if she stayed their game would no longer be an innocent one. To that foolish, feminine part of her that had wanted to stay and damn the consequences, she muttered a fierce warning. Although Simon might not be aware of it, she knew quite well that she was not his sexual equal; that she was not accustomed to indulging in the sensual play of people who became lovers for no better reason than that it suited the mood of the moment. Another woman, more experienced than she was herself, would no doubt have stayed and thereby implicitly invited more intimate lovemaking, knowing it for what it was—simply a different stage in a different game with no emotional meaning to it—a simple but sophisticated satisfying of an appetite that was purely sexual, but she did not have that experience and for her to invite Simon's lovemaking was eventually to betray to him the fact that she was still a virgin.

There were conclusions to be drawn from that which she had no wish for him to draw. They had established a good working rapport—professionally she found him stimulating and she was already so involved in Kit Masterson's story that not to see it through would cause her acute disappointment. For Simon to discover she was still a virgin would alter the axis of their relationship completely. He had said that once he believed she had been ready to barter her virginity for a wedding ring; he might suspect her of trying to trap him again.

She could acknowledge now, with a fierce pang of

anguish, that she still wanted him as her lover. There was such a powerful air of male sensuality about him that she doubted many women would not. If things were different; if she were not a virgin, it would be easy to give rein to that desire. She was no longer naïve enough to confuse desire with love and was perfectly able to see that the one could exist independently of the other. Not so very long ago her mother had remarked frankly that it was a pity that the men one normally desired were not the same ones who deserved to be loved; and it was true. But since she could hardly go to Simon and say, 'Look, I'm still a virgin, and I want you to make love to me but that doesn't mean I love you,' she would simply have to ignore or control her sexual response to him. Without the past between them her virginity need not have been a barrier. She smiled wryly to herself, spreading out one of the towels to lie on, thinking of all the men she had known since Simon and who would have jumped at the chance of being her lover. Up until now she had thought herself wise in denying them. Mere attraction had never seemed a strong enough motive to make love with them, but had she not done so, she would be free now ... It must be something to do with the sun, she decided drowsily, lying on her stomach, her head pillowed on her arms; it must be bringing out a latent vein of sensuality in her.

She was aware of Simon coming to stand beside her, although she didn't turn over. He took the other towel and spread it out next to hers, lying down beside her.

'Still not hungry?'

She shook her head without looking at him.

'I'd say I was more inclined to be sleepy. Disgraceful, isn't it?'

'Well if you're going to sleep, you'd better have some oil on your skin first.'

She could sense that Simon had moved, but a lazy inertia seemed to possess her, and although she lifted her head to watch him removing a bottle of sun oil from the basket she made no attempt to move or to protest when he kneeled over her, pouring some of the fluid on to her back, slowly smoothing it over her skin.

'Why don't you take this off?' His fingers touched the fastening of her bikini. 'If you don't you'll only end up with strap marks. The beach is completely private. No one's going to see,' he added, almost as though he could feel the tension suddenly gripping her.

He was going to see . . . And yet Christy knew that to protest would be ridiculous. She often sunbathed topless in the privacy of the garden at home, discreetly perhaps, but topless nevertheless, and to object simply because she was not alone was hardly likely to convince Simon of her supposed sophistication. The continental beaches were full of girls who wouldn't care less who looked at them, and yet it was because Simon *wasn't* a stranger that she felt this inner coiling of apprehension mixed with excitement. She wanted to do as he suggested, she acknowledged inwardly, and more, she wanted the slow stroke of his hands on her body smoothing away all the barriers until there was only the silken touch of skin against skin.

He's simply talking about sunbathing, she reminded herself, calling a halt to her rioting thoughts; simply making a suggestion that he considered practical and if she lingered too long in replying to him *she* would be the one who was being provocative.

Glad that he wasn't able to see her face, she murmured. 'Mm. I think I will,' and made to sit up, keeping her back to him, but his hand on her back kept her where she was. 'I'll do it for you.'

He unfastened the clip deftly, and gave the stretch fabric a brief tug, so that she was forced to lift her body slightly to allow him to pull her top away. Once he had done so he simply returned to his original task of smoothing the oil over her skin, making no attempt to touch the exposed sides of her breasts.

'Did you do any sunbathing in India?'

His question surprised her, but then her skin was already quite dark, it tanned easily and they had had a good spring and summer—working for her mother at home meant that she was able to arrange her time to take the maximum advantage of the good weather and perhaps he thought her tan a residue of the one she had got the previous year.

'Not really, the pace was too hectic and the heat wasn't the sunbathing type.'

'You and Miles stayed up in the hills for a couple of months didn't you?'

'Yes.' He seemed remarkably well informed about their trip. 'That was after Miles had completed his research. He rented a bungalow there because he felt that the feel of the place helped with the book—more so than if he'd returned to England to write. It was a delightful place, part of an original hill station. I enjoyed it.'

His hand had reached the base of her spine and for some reason its pressure hardened. Her bikini bottom tied with fabric bows and his hand moved under one. 'Do you want to take this off as well? I warn you I'm going to dispense with my shorts; the combination of wet denim encrusted with salt against my skin isn't exactly pleasant.' He was already unfastening the small bow, taking her silence for assent and once again Christy reminded herself that there was nothing sexual in his actions. He had already told her that he swam nude and in fact had she been alone on this paradise of a beach wouldn't she quite naturally have sunbathed and swum nude herself?

As the first bow slackened she felt him reach over and unfasten the other. Her bottom wasn't as brown as the rest of her. Although the vicarage gardens were private enough and large enough for her to be able to fasten her top before any unexpected visitor could find her, Harry's habit of arriving to do the garden at any odd moment that took his fancy had meant that she had been slightly wary of stripping off altogether.

When Simon moved slightly away without attempting to remove the triangles of cotton that formed her briefs, she wasn't sure whether disappointment or relief was uppermost. If she had needed confirmation that his suggestion was not sexually motivated she had surely just got it. He had his back to her when he stepped out of his shorts, his actions so matter of fact that they made her realise just how accustomed he was to the intimacy of male and female nudity. By the time he settled back on his towel, she had removed her bikini bottoms and was lying down on her stomach once more, her head turned slightly to one side and her eyes closed, but within what seemed like minutes she was already uncomfortably conscious of the prickle of heat on her exposed rear, and she knew that unless she wanted to burn she would have to put some oil on it.

'What's the matter?'

Simon must have sensed her irritation, because he reached out and removed her sunglasses, his eyes vividly gold as they stared into hers.

'It's nothing. I think I'll put some more oil on. I don't want to burn.'

He glanced down over her body and then grinned. 'Umm, I see what you mean. I'll do it for you,' he offered, 'save you having to struggle.' She wanted to refuse, but if she did he might think it odd. He got up lazily and her eyes skimmed helplessly over his body. Unlike hers, his tan was even, his body sleekly male, smooth brown skin covering hard muscle and bone.

She turned away resting her forehead on her hands praying that he wouldn't realise what a devastating effect he had on her. Her nipples ached, suddenly sensitive to the rough fabric of the towel, her stomach tense.

'Umm ... very sexy ...' She could hear the faint thread of laughter in his voice as he traced the demarcation line between her tan and the paler skin and her body quivered. A desire to turn over and invite the intimacy of his touch surged through her and she struggled to overcome it, inwardly deriding herself for her lack of self-control, 'I take it you don't make a habit of sunbathing in the nude?'

'The garden at home's scarcely the most private place in the world,' Christy reminded him, trying to match his lazy humour. 'And old Harry's renowned for his earthy sense of humour—in addition to being the village gossip.'

'Umm, I see what you mean. But Miles has a pool at that place of his in Surrey.'

Rather surprised that he should think she saw enough of Miles to make herself at home in his house, she simply said, 'Yes . . .' and then subsided into a tense silence as she felt the smooth stroke of his hand over her buttocks. It seemed an age before his hand moved to her thigh and when he eventually moved away completely she felt rather like a child who had successfully endured a trip to the dentist without disgracing herself. In those days she seemed to remember her mother had rewarded her with some little treat. If she were offered a treat now . . . She was glad Simon couldn't see her face. This was completely ridiculous. Never in her life had she experienced such a fierce surge of desire, such a need to touch and caress another human being. Not even at eighteen had she experienced desire as intense as this. She was quite relieved when she opened her eyes to find that Simon was lying on his stomach with his face turned away from her, but then to her consternation she heard herself saying huskily. 'Would you like me to return the favour? You could burn . . .'

She saw the ripple of tension grip his spine. He didn't move and his voice was curiously harsh as he muttered curtly, 'No . . . no . . . I'm fine.'

It was ridiculous to have to suppress the hurt sting of tears filming her eyes simply because he had made it plain he didn't want her to touch him, but she was having to do so. He had said that he still desired her but his curt rejection conveyed a different message. Christy closed her eyes, willing her body to relax into sleep, unaware of the moment reality took over from pretence, just as she was unaware of the way Simon looked at her when he was at liberty to do so without being observed.

It was Simon shaking her shoulder that finally roused her. While she slept he had moved the umbrella so that her head lay in the shade, and as she blinked sleepily she heard him saying, 'I had to wake you, if you lie there much longer you'll fry, oil or no oil.'

Still half asleep she moved lazily, conscious of a pleasurable awareness of her own body, a freedom which was both unexpected and sensual. She turned on her side, stretching luxuriously as she smiled at him, her smile frozen by the look in his eyes.

'Christy!' Her name sounded thick and unfamiliar, his hand moving unsteadily from her shoulder to move in a caressing sweep from her breast to her thigh and then back again to enclose her breast. She had no thought of rejecting him; the delight engendered by his touch was too closely entwined with her own sun- and sleep-induced sensuality. Instead she stretched languidly beneath his caress, murmuring softly with pleasure. She had forgotten that he didn't want her to touch him and reached out automatically, feathering her fingertips along the dark line of hairs arrowing down his body. She felt his stomach muscles clench beneath her touch and heard his muttered exclamation. He had been kneeling by her side while he tried to wake her, but now he lay down, smoothing both hands down over her back, shaping her to him. 'Perhaps I should have let you put that oil on me after all,' he murmured against her lips, teasing them with brief kisses, 'but touching you had got me so damned aroused . . .'

So that was why he had been so curt with her? His

admission came as a revelation. Somehow although he had admitted desiring her she had felt that he, unlike her, possessed some super-human power that made him able to control his desires in a way that she could not. 'I promise you that when I brought you here I didn't plan for this to happen.' His mouth was still taking teasing bites from hers, tantalising and tormenting her, making her ache for the pleasure of his mouth against her own. Her arms were wrapped around him her hips arching wantonly against him, her legs entrapped by his.

'And now that it has?'

'I'd be a fool not to take what the fates are offering. Six years ago the time wasn't right for us, but now . . . Did you feel like this with Miles?'

The question stunned her. What on earth could she say? She supposed it was natural enough for a man to want to be praised for his prowess; for his ability to arouse and pleasure. She could tell him that she and Miles had never made love, but then he might guess the truth and if he did . . . A reckless tide of feeling surged through her and she smiled into his eyes, threading her fingers through his dark hair and said teasingly, 'Who's Miles? I can't seem to remember.'

Her answer seemed to appease him, although his eyes were still faintly shadowed, almost as though he suffered some sort of pain. Her body, so closely entwined with his, ached for more than teasing kisses, and she reached up impulsively towards him, using her teeth to tug slowly on his bottom lip, running her tongue lightly over his top one, finding within herself an instinctive sensuality she had never known she possessed, her breasts hardening provocatively against the wall of his chest, her hands running lightly over his back, holding him to her, until the shadow disappeared and his mouth locked over hers, his hands twining in her hair to hold her still beneath the slow, deliberate ravishment of his kiss. For a long time they did nothing but that, kissing one another with deliberate appreciation, until the languid intimacy of their mouths stopped being sensually satisfying and instead became a mutually unendurable form of refined torment that their bodies registered and protested against in growing waves of urgency.

'My God, you're unbelievable.' Simon lifted his mouth from hers to whisper the words thickly in her ear. 'Beautiful, beautiful Christy.' He lifted himself away from her slightly and ran his hand the length of her body, watching her with an intensity that burned dark gold in the tawny depths of his eyes. 'Touch me, kiss me.' His hands gripped her wrists, a hoarse sound of pleasure shuddering through him as she placed her hands palms down on his chest and then started to caress him with slow, languid movements, feeling the urgent thud of his heart, breathing in the warm, male musky scent of him as her lips caressed the taut column of his throat, her tongue teasing its rigid male outline. She felt him shudder, his hands gripping her hips, the aroused pressure of his body against her own intensely exciting. She was in the grip of an unfamiliar fever; its urgency so compelling that there was room for nothing else. Her body seemed to know instinctively how to move against Simon's, teasing and inciting, his growled male protest at her torment feeding her excitement.

'Want to play games do you?' he muttered mock

menacingly in her ear. His teeth enclosing the lobe in
erotic stimulation, his hands cupped her breasts and
he lifted himself away from her, studying the golden
orbs of flesh with their darker crowns. As though she
were a puppet manipulated by strings which he
controlled, Christy found herself arching pleadingly
under his scrutiny; and then gasping with pleasure as
his thumbs brushed their aroused, thrusting peaks.
Her breasts had always been what she considered to be
slightly over-full, but Simon seemed to find no fault
with them, murmuring softly encouraging words of
praise as they responded with wanton pleasure to his
caresses.

Need coiled and ached in the pit of her stomach, his
name leaving her throat on a soft cry.

'Ah no . . . not yet,' he denied her rawly. 'You were
the one who wanted to play.' His head came down, his
tongue brushing circles of burning fire round her
nipples. Her body arched and tensed welcoming the
fierce heat of Simon's touch as his hand stroked over
her stomach. His tongue touched her nipple and she
cried out achingly, her fingers curling feverishly into
his hair as she arched against him, her thighs parting
in a wave of shivering urgency that demanded more
than the delicate exploration of his hand. Her sharp
cry seemed to unleash a corresponding need in him
and his mouth closed over her nipple, waves of
sensation so acutely pleasurable that they could
scarcely be borne radiating over her body as she
succumbed to the sensual tug of his mouth and the
slow experienced stroke of his fingers. When he
suddenly stopped touching her Christy felt like death,
confused and almost ill with rejection and frustration.

'It's the 'phone,' he told her tersely and sure enough Christy realising that the ringing sound she could hear was not in her head but coming from the top of the cliff.

'Someone will appear in a moment if I don't go and answer it ... It's the arrangement I have with Helen. No one rings me here unless it's important. God ...' He turned his back on her while he pulled on his shorts. 'What a time to ring.'

'I'll come back with you ... I think I've had enough sun for one day.' Now that he had stopped touching her, suddenly she was released from the powerful tug of desire that had controlled her. She felt faint and shaky with the enormity of what had so nearly happened. If they hadn't been interrupted he would have made love to her completely and then what?

She sensed the question in his look and said shakily, 'I think we both got rather carried away ...'

'And you've just realised that for you and I to become lovers isn't a good idea.' Simon broke in with savage contempt. 'Oh yes I know exactly what's going through your mind,' he told her, 'but you can't deny that you wanted me.' He frowned as the 'phone continued to ring, and said curtly, 'We'll discuss this later,' before loping off into the direction of the steps.

Christy followed him at a more leisurely pace, still thrown off balance by the intensity of her sexual response to him. She would have to be doubly on her guard from now on. Simon was a very sensual man; her's was the only female companionship he was likely to have in the immediate future and it was only natural that that should increase his desire for her. Somehow she would have to find a way of keeping him at bay, and her own feelings under control.

And reluctant though she was to admit it, she sensed that the latter task would be the harder.

CHAPTER SIX

AT first it was hard, and Christy did not miss the angry gleam in Simon's eyes when she endeavoured to make sure they were never left alone, but then the fates seemed to take pity on her, and after almost two days of increasing tension she was awakened one morning by Helen shaking her quickly, to tell her in her Caribbean mixture of French and English that Simon was waiting for her downstairs and that she was to pack enough clothes to cover her for a couple of days.

When she got downstairs, Simon had already had his breakfast, his manner so brisk and businesslike that it was impossible to imagine him as an importuning lover.

'That 'phone call the other day was the weather bureau. From what they said, and by my reckoning the next couple of days will be almost perfect for diving. We'll leave just as soon as you're ready. Our suits and equipment are already on board *Stormsurf* and Georges is standing by to drive us over to the harbour.'

Once she realised what was happening Christy was almost too excited to eat. Over the last couple of days she had spent a good deal of time talking to Pierre about Kit Masterson and the legend of his death, as much to keep out of Simon's way as anything else, but all that she had learned from the old man had reinforced her earlier fascination and now she was almost as eager as Simon to get out to the reef.

It hadn't taken her long to pack—shorts and shirts, clean underwear, a pair of jeans and two thick sweaters just in case it became cold, that was all she would need for their brief stay on board *Stormsurf*. Protective clothing and their diving gear was already on board, and her senses tingled with anticipation as she sat beside Simon in the narrow confines of the old Land-Rover.

His staff knew about his proposed dive, he had already told her, but they had been asked to keep it secret. 'Tourists visit the island, although admittedly only in small numbers,' he had explained, 'I don't want to find that *Stormsurf* is surrounded by half a dozen or more pleasure craft—for one thing the waters round there are just too dangerous for inexperienced sailors.'

Christy could quite understand his point of view and it was with relief that she saw that the small harbour was empty apart from the elegant white shape of *Stormsurf*.

Although the harbour was privately owned and went with the house Simon had told her that the rights to it were shared by the other villa owners in the area, who often let their properties to holidaymakers during the busy season.

The constraint there had been between them during the last two days vanished completely as they worked efficiently together to get *Stormsurf* moving. It was still early enough in the morning for the sea to be almost perfectly calm, although Christy could see the odd breaker rolling beyond the lagoon.

'It will take us about three hours to get out to our diving spot,' Simon told Christy as he headed for the natural break in the coral. 'I have checked over the diving gear, but you might do it again if you will. We can't afford to take any chances.'

Christy did as he asked, wondering if he had made the request because he wanted her out of his way. He had made no reference to what had happened down on the beach, but when in those first tormented twenty-four hours afterwards, she had not allowed him to do, making sure she was too busy to have time to speak personally with him. But even if they did talk about it what could they say? She now knew that Simon desired her physically and that, if the circumstances promoted it, he would be likely to make love to her, but no matter how much the newly discovered sensual side of her nature might incline her to want him to there was still the hurdle of her virginity. She could see all manner of complications arising from Simon's discovery of it; there would be guilt, possibly recriminations and an atmosphere between them that would destroy whatever pleasure there had been in their being lovers. Simon had accused her of trying to trap him into marriage once, and that accusation still stung. The diving equipment checked, she turned her attention to the supplies in the small galley, repressing a faintly self-mocking grimace as she dwelt on the injustice of discovering that the first man she met who could make her body ache for the possession of his, independently of whatever she thought in her mind, should also be the one man she would be wise not to get involved with.

When she had inspected everything she possibly

could below decks, she went back topside, pausing for a moment to study the back view of Simon's male outline as he stood behind the wheel. He was wearing his faded denim cut-off shorts and nothing else, his body burned a rich dark brown, his dark hair tousled by the breeze. Trickles of awareness slithered down her spine as Christy watched him. He was all male power and grace; a subtle mixture that fascinated and yet repelled in the same way that one was drawn to the savage beauty of the hunters of the animal world. As though sensing her presence he turned and looked at her. For a moment neither of them spoke, and Christy knew with a deeply rooted feminine instinct that if he had come to her then she would not have been able to resist him. But of course he could not come to her; he had to navigate the ketch.

'Only another hour now. We'll drop anchor and then I'll make the first dive.'

He didn't say anything else, and Christy did not go over to join him by the wheel. Instead she sat down on the deck, watching the water skim by, momentarily entranced by a school of dolphins, as different from sharks as white from black—good from evil; happy, peaceful creatures as loved by man almost as much as sharks were hated. They with their great intelligence had no desire to kill and maim and yet in many ways because of their peace-loving natures they were vulnerable. Perhaps as with man they needed a little of the shark's natural aggression in order to survive.

They were well outside the reef now, and Christy felt it the moment the ketch turned towards the point, the effect of the powerful cross-currents below the surface, ruffling the ketch's smooth progress. Even today with the winds and currents in their favour she could feel the power that lurked beneath the surface and she shuddered to imagine what it would be like to be the captain of a craft like Kit Masterson's faced with the full fury of a Caribbean storm. He would have needed skill; and faith, not just in God but in his own abilities, and his attention for one moment deflected ... perhaps as it had been on that fearful night when he realised there was no familiar light shining from Isabella's bedroom window ... Shivering, Christy looked away from the sea, chiding herself for her over-active imagination. She must put a curb on these foolish daydreams, especially when she was diving. Diving ... excitement had given way to faint trepidation, and she admitted inwardly to herself that without the security of Simon's skill and support she doubted that she would have felt confident to make the dive. Was that why she was so powerfully attracted to him sexually? Because deep down inside herself, against her will, against everything she knew about him, some part of her insisted on placing in him the blind faith of an adoring teenager? Not wanting to pursue the thought any further she paced the deck restlessly until she realised they had reached their destination.

Beyond the boiling surf she could see the peace of the lagoon, but to reach it one would have to brave those cruelly sharp teeth of coral she could just see protruding above the foam-flecked sea.

'We'll anchor here. Can you come and hold the wheel for a moment?' She did as Simon requested, feeling the fierce tug of the current as she obeyed his instruction. Once they were secured by the strong sea anchors the tug diminished, but it was still there, she reminded herself, shivering a little. Because it had been tamed by man's inventions that didn't mean it was totally controlled.

'Keep an eye on things up here while I go down and get ready will you?' Simon asked. 'There shouldn't be any problems, but there's no point in taking risks.'

This was the other side of him; the side that had been tempered in the melting pot of life, and Christy respected it. He was barely gone for ten minutes, emerging from below clad in a black wet-suit, holding his oxygen tanks in one hand. While he put them on Christy watched him, admiring the skilled economy of his movements. He was a man who, whatever he did, he would have to do well and she shivered a little remembering how her body yearned to have him as its lover. In that too he would be skilled and knowledgeable.

His preparations over, he looked at his watch and said curtly to Christy. 'Time check?' When they had synchronised their watches, he pointed to the support line he had clipped round his waist.

'If I haven't made contact in an hour, three tugs on this will remind me how long I've been down. If I find anything, I'll give one tug; if I run into any problems and I'm in difficulty I'll give two. Okay?

Christy watched as he slid neatly below the boiling surface, all her attention concentrated on the spot where he had disappeared. For a moment the acute sense of desolation she experienced shocked her. She was a fairly experienced diver—experienced enough for Simon to believe she was quite capable of handling this type of dive—and yet she was behaving like a complete amateur. As the minutes slipped by her sense of loss eased; she was able to monitor the movements of the ketch as well as keeping an eye on the line. Occasionally a fiercer tug than those she was used to on the ketch's anchors reminded her of the power lurking beneath the turquoise blue surface.

Promptly, just on the hour, without her needing to remind him, Simon surfaced. Christy waited until he was on board, and rid of his oxygen tanks before she questioned him.

'I'm convinced there's something there,' he told her, 'but whether it's Kit Masterson's ship or not, I can't tell until I'm able to remove enough coral to bring up something that can be tested and dated. That's one of the reasons I was so keen to have you with me. I've explored right along the coral, and I'm convinced I can make out the definite line of a hull. I'm not going to tell you exactly where, I want you to see it for yourself and then sketch it for me.'

His words brought back all Christy's original excitement. Suddenly she couldn't wait to see what he was describing for herself.

When Simon answered 'after lunch' in response to her enquiry as to when she could go down, she was bitterly disappointed. 'But if I eat, I'll have to wait at least a couple of hours. I'm not at all hungry, I could go down now.'

Simon seemed to consider. 'Well if you're sure,' he said at last. 'But remember, the first hint of any problem, and you come back up. That was what we agreed.'

Now it was her turn to go below and don her wet

suit. The familiarity of it close to her skin enclosed her in a different world, she could almost taste the chlorine and hear the voice of her first diving instructor.

Up on deck Simon insisted on checking her tanks before he helped her on with the heavy equipment. For a moment as she waited on the deck apprehension quivered along her spine and then it was submerged by the tide of tingling excitement racing along her veins.

'Ready?'

She nodded briefly, securing the line round her waist, all her attention concentrated on what she was doing

'Christy . . .' There was a note in Simon's voice she didn't recognise; something almost approaching concern. 'No heroics,' he warned her soberly, and then his tone changing to brisk efficiency, he gave her a cool nod. 'Okay then if you're ready.'

The initial shock of the water as she slid beneath the waves disorientated her, but only for a moment. The sea was so crystal clear and pure that she had to remind herself to take it slowly, the clarity of the water making the depth deceptive. Luckily they weren't having to dive to dangerous depths, but no diver ever took risks with the unpleasant spectre of the terrible diver's disease, 'the bends' as it was known, always hovering over them. For diving to these depths they did not need a decompression chamber, but nevertheless caution was always necessary, and so Christy dived slowly, pausing occasionally to study the delicacy of the coral face, fascinated by its apparent frailty, and yet knowing that for all its delicacy it could rip the bottom out of an unsuspecting boat as easily as she could slit open an envelope.

Tiny brilliantly coloured schools of fish darted past her, weaving in and out of the coral face. Below her she could see the sandy bottom and now, also, she could feel the fierce surge of the cross currents, and was glad of her supporting line. It would be easy to be distracted by this fascinating underwater world and swept away by those dangerous currents before one realised what was happening.

She was down here to do a job she reminded herself, almost breathless with delight as she watched the antics of a school of angel fish, longing intensely for her pencil and pad. Simon had told her that he had already taken photographs, but no one photograph could take in all that he wanted to show and so the elusive character of the lines he was hoping to discover beneath the coral were lost.

Manoeuvring herself carefully Christy examined the coral face, emptying her mind of preconceived ideas and concentrating instead on letting the shape of it become absorbed into her concentration.

Yes, she could see how this might easily have once been the hull of some ship. Excitement quickened along her veins as she swam slowly to and fro, studying one particular outcrop from several angles. Simon had not told her exactly where she would find Kit's ship, but she was sure that this was it. Coral had covered whatever was left of it, but the shape of a hull was almost unmistakable. Her fingers ached to tug and pull it away and discover what lay beneath, but she knew that would be almost impossible. Great skill and care would be required for such a task. A ship the size of Kit's, well-loaded down with men and their possessions, must have possessed dozens of artefacts which must lie here somewhere, buried in the sand and coral. She went down to the sea bed, disturbing small sea creatures as she set up spurts of sand. Lumps of coral and debris lay everywhere. A sensation of desperation overwhelmed her. There must be something here that would confirm Simon's theory, if she could only find it. A guilty glance at her watch showed her that her hour was nearly up. It had seemed only minutes since she came down here—that was the fascination and the danger of an underwater world. Reluctantly she started to swim back to the surface, her mind full of images and colours.

Simon was waiting to help her back on deck. 'Well?' he asked when he had helped her strip off her tanks.

'I think I found it.' She described to him what she had seen and he nodded. 'Umm ... that's what I think. Can you draw it from memory?'

'I should think so. It's a pity you don't have any drawings of Kit's ship. That would give an interesting comparison.

'I do.' His grin caught her unawares, momentarily stunning her into forgetting everything but her need to reach out and touch him; to trace the curving warmth of his male mouth and then to press her fingers to it. Anticipation tingled through her, swiftly controlled as she realised where her errant thoughts were leading. 'Well, not exactly Kit's ship.' Simon amended, apparently unaware of what she was experiencing, 'but one of the same class. I checked with the admiralty and they had some drawings dating from the time and were kind enough to let me photograph them. They're in the main cabin.'

'Why didn't you tell me about them before?' Christy asked him as she followed him down, too excited to be aware of any discomfort from her wet-suit.

'Because I want to see what you produce first,' he told her calmly. 'You must have a rough idea of what a vessel of that time looked like. I want you to produce a drawing for me based on what you've seen underwater, using that as a guide-line towards size and so on so that I can compare it with my drawings.'

He was setting her a difficult task, and yet it was one she could feel herself responding to. She couldn't wait to get started, and as though he sensed her anticipation Simon said, 'Lunch first though. You go and get out of those wet things and I'll get it ready.'

He was no mere stereotyped macho male, Christy thought ten minutes later showering briskly, reflecting on how few men of her acquaintance would have so readily assumed the domestic role.

When she emerged from her cabin, washed and dressed, Simon was in the galley cooking a delicious-looking omelette.

'I thought you'd prefer something light,' he told her. 'Go and sit down, I'll bring it through in a second.'

It was obvious that he had everything under control; she could smell the rich aroma of freshly brewed coffee and in the main salon she found that the table had been set, a plate of tempting crusty bread and a bowl of fruit waiting in readiness.

Simon's omelette tasted every bit as good as it looked. Christy ate hers hungrily, pausing when she realised that Simon was watching her. His scrutiny made her colour slightly. 'Something wrong?'

'No, I was just thinking that six years haven't changed you that much after all. You always did have a healthy appetite. Miles is something of a picky eater as I remember.'

Christy wasn't sure why he had brought that up. It was true that Miles, as an only child, had grown up to be rather fussy about his food, and it had been something that had occasionally annoyed her in India, but she had learned to cope with it.

Now she gave a brief shrug. 'Why should Miles' eating habits worry me?'

Simon didn't answer her first, simply giving her a rather enigmatic look, before drawling laconically, 'Why, indeed?'

It was as though a barrier had suddenly come between them; the warm camaraderie they had just shared suddenly transmuted into a totally unexpected veiled hostility. Gone was the intelligent, instructive companion Simon had been that morning and in his place was the laconic, mocking male who had first approached her about this venture. Simon was as dangerous and changeable as the Caribbean itself, she thought crossly, refusing to let him bait her into any unwise comments, as he taunted her with sardonic comments about Miles and their work together in India.

What could it possibly matter to him whether or not she had slept with Miles she reflected inwardly, when she realised the direction his jibes were taking. For her own self-preservation she deemed it sensible to allow him to think that they had. It would never do for him to guess the truth—not in this mood.

'Tell me?' he demanded in a lazy drawl when they had both finished eating, 'is it part of your policy to have a sexual relationship with all the men you work with?' Without waiting for her to answer, he continued insultingly, 'It certainly proved a bonus to Miles. I understand some of the passages in his new book are almost erotic.'

She wouldn't deign to tell him that it had been her idea that Miles included a romantic element in his novel or that Miles had been inspired to do so after their visit to a remote shrine one ruler had built in memory of his love for the daughter of a British merchant who had lived beneath his protection. Miles was not a highly sexually motivated man. Originally a university don, he had confided to Christy that as a boy he had contemplated entering the priesthood and she could well imagine him being suited to such a celibate life. A successful writer was a definite matrimonial catch, but Christy had never heard of him being intensely romantically involved. However, she was not going to admit any of this to Simon. Let him make as much fun of her and Miles as he wished, she was not going to respond to his taunting.

However, it was with great difficulty that she held on to her temper when he said softly, 'Tell me . . . are you as passionately responsive to him as you are to me?'

It was an unexpected question and one she could not in honesty answer, so instead, she merely compressed her mouth and said pointedly, 'I haven't questioned you about your personal life, Simon.'

His mouth twisted, and if she hadn't known better she might have suspected it was bitterness that twisted

its well-shaped outline. 'No, you haven't have you?'
He stood up then, pushing his chair back with a rare
awkwardness. 'If you've finished, I suggest you get on
with your drawings. I'm going to go and get some
weather checks, with a bit of luck I might manage to
get another dive in before it goes dark.'

She ought to have been pleased that he was leaving
her alone to work, but instead she felt restless, unable
to settle, her mind and emotions too keyed up for her
to be able to concentrate properly, but gradually she
was able to recapture the mood of excitement that had
gripped her underwater, her fingers deftly reproducing
the images relayed to her by her mind so that the coral
wall gradually began to take shape on the paper in
front of her.

Only when her task was completed to her
satisfaction did she turn her mind to the other
challenge Simon had set her. For several minutes she
simply studied what she had already drawn, and then
slowly she allowed other images to fill her mind; her
imagination slowly stripping away the coral to reveal
Kit's ship as she must once have been. Only when a
definite picture had formed in her mind did she reach
for fresh paper but once she had begun she started to
sketch with an almost feverish intensity; working
almost too fast to be aware of what was taking shape in
front of her.

When Simon suddenly walked into the cabin
wearing his wet-suit it took her several seconds to drag
her attention away from what she was doing. When
she did she glanced frowningly at her watch, stunned
to discover how long she had been working.

'I'm going down now,' Simon told her tersely,

without showing any interest in her work. 'I won't be more than an hour.'

Following his example Christy checked her watch, and then followed him up on deck to watch him strap on fresh air cylinders and drop gracefully overboard while she tried to quell a surge of disappointment that he hadn't asked to see what she had done.

While he was gone she decided to work on deck so that she could keep a check on his safety line. After half an hour she was satisfied that she had done as much as much as she could and, stretching her tense fingers, she studied her own drawing, half surprised by the amount of detail she had managed to put into the small sketch. Who would have believed her memory could retain so much extraneous detail, although she suspected what she had drawn was probably more Hollywood's vision of how an Elizabethan vessel should look, than the Admiralty's. Shrugging she went below decks to put the drawings safely in the main cabin, not stopping to linger there, mindful of her responsibility towards Simon. A brief glance at her watch showed her that he had fifteen minutes more to go and she sat down close to the line, having checked that the sea anchors were still holding them firm. During the afternoon the wind had changed direction and although its freshness was welcome in the enervating heat, she was concerned that the change in the weather might herald unworkable conditions for them to dive in.

When Simon had been down five minutes over his hour she checked her watch carefully, and then reached for the life-line giving the prearranged signal. She knew how easy it was for one to misjudge time when underwater, and felt no particular alarm until Simon failed to respond to her signal. She waited another five minutes, all of which passed with excruciating slowness, before tugging again, but when she touched the line it was disconcertingly slack, and fear trembled through her, visions of Simon being attacked by a shark, perhaps in other equally dangerous difficulties, flooding through her. She was just on the point of going for her her own wet-suit when he broke the surface several yards away, swimming powerfully towards the ketch, the loose line held in one hand.

Although she was tense with apprehension Christy waited until he was on board and had tugged off his oxygen cylinders before questioning him.

'The line snagged on some coral,' he told her. 'I thought I wasn't going to be able to get it free so I unclipped it. That's what delayed me.'

'I gave the signal but you didn't respond.'

'I managed to work it free, but lost hold of it. That's when you must have tugged. Nothing to panic about,' he told her laconically, adding roughly, 'Stop looking so concerned—you might give me ideas.'

Too over-wrought to monitor her own reactions, Christy demanded rawly, 'What sort of ideas?' Tears weren't very far away, a revelation so disturbing and unexpected, shattering her peace of mind that it was all she could do not to get up and run as far away from him as she could. In those few seconds before he had surfaced she had been awash with fear for him—and not merely the fear anyone would have for the safety of a friend or companion, but the fear of a woman for the man she loves. She still loved Simon! Strangely enough she was not shocked. It was almost as though some part of her had always known the truth. Was this why she had feared to come with him; why she had hidden her feelings away behind a wall of bitterness and anger . . . why she had responded so passionately to his touch?

'What's the matter, Simon?' she demanded harshly, lashing herself into a state of anger, intent on protecting herself and her vulnerability from him. 'I already know that you like to walk alone . . . Just because I'm worried about you doesn't mean that I'm still an adolescent, stupid enough to fall in love with you.'

Just for a moment she was frightened that her very denial might have betrayed her, but Simon's expression reassured her. His face had closed up, his mouth tight and angry. 'If you want someone to worry about try worrying about your friend Miles,' he told her grittily. 'He's the one who'll appreciate nursemaiding—not me. I don't need a mother substitute, Christy . . . nor do I want to play mock-father. I want a woman I can meet on equal terms.'

'You mean someone who's prepared to accept sex in the place of love,' Christy threw at him bitterly, too blindly caught up in the anger that seemed to be consuming them both to be concerned about what she was saying. It seemed impossible to believe that they were quarrelling like this . . . that the friendship and respect she had believed was growing between them could be so easily destroyed. How false it really must have been . . .

'I'm going below to get changed,' she told him thickly. 'With a bit of luck there might be time for me to get in one more dive. I want to look at that coral formation again.'

His mouth compressed. 'It's too late for that today. While I was down there I thought I felt the current pick up. It looks as though the weather might be changing faster than I'd hoped. I need to get further weather checks, so we'll call it a day now.'

Christy knew that he was speaking sensibly, even so she longed to escape from his presence. The discovery that she still loved him had knocked her off balance. She needed time to come to terms with it ... to explore her feelings and readjust her own perceptions of herself. How had she managed to deceive herself so thoroughly that she was over him? Why had she never suspected that her denial of any feelings for him had been too vehement? Perhaps because she hadn't wanted to, she admitted, going down to the galley intent on busying herself with some preparations for their evening meal.

She heard Simon come down to the main cabin, and then go through to his own room. The shower ran and she imagined him standing beneath it the water glistening over his tanned skin. Tremors shook her body, her hand shaking so much that she could only lean against the tiny sink, willing herself to find some measure of self-control. Dear God, why couldn't she have discovered how she felt *before* she had agreed to come to the Caribbean? If she had suffered before at eighteen, it was nothing to what she was going to suffer now. It would be so easy to go to him and tempt him into making love to her ... part of her craved the physical satisfaction that would bring with it a wildness she barely recognised as belonging to her, but there was a reverse side to that coin; there was pain and rejection and the inevitable self-contempt she must suffer in knowing that it was not purely his physical lovemaking she wanted. Before, she had loved him as an adolescent; content almost to worship and adore, now she loved him with all the sharp pain of a woman. She shuddered deeply, fighting for composure as she heard his door opening.

She sensed his presence behind her without turning her head. 'Christy, these drawings . . .' She sensed a note of wonder in his voice and dared to turn round, wishing she hadn't when she realised how close to her he actually was. 'Stop what you're doing,' he commanded her, 'and come in here.'

Mutely she followed him into the main salon, and stood watching as he opened a drawer and removed a roll of photographs. 'Now, look at these,' he commanded softly. The trauma of her own feelings became of secondary consideration as she studied what he had put in front of her. Almost detail for detail the photographs and the sketches she had done matched . . .

'It's . . . it's almost unbelievable . . .'

'It's more than that . . . It's a bloody miracle.' His hands grasped her waist as he swung her round almost lifting her off her feet. 'Christy. Christy it's a break-through . . . What you've drawn convinces me that I'm on the right track . . . that that is Kit Masterson's ship down there. All we need now is some actual physical proof.'

She could feel his tense excitement . . . catch his euphoric mood as the man gave way to the writer, totally absorbed in his work. She wanted him to be right, she admitted inwardly, and not just because she, too, was caught up in the excitement of proving the legend of Kit Masterson, but also for his own sake.

The excitement suddenly died from his eyes and he studied her almost broodingly. She sensed that he was about to kiss her and much as she longed for the warm possession of his mouth against her own she had enough instinct for self-preservation left to pull back from him.

'Ah no . . . I forgot . . . your kisses are all reserved for Miles, aren't they?'

It was almost as though he was waiting for her to deny it, but caution warned her not to do so. Let him think she was involved with Miles if that would stop him from wanting to make love to her. It was safer that way, she told herself bleakly, turning away without vouchsaving him any answer, other than a cool, 'I'd better go and get on with dinner . . . I expect you'll want an early start in the morning.'

She was relieved when he took his cue from her, although she mistrusted the sardonic twist of his mouth that accompanied his laconic affirmative. This wouldn't be the first time Simon had shared the ketch with a woman, and a knife-like jab of jealousy stabbed through her as she imagined what it would be like to be one of the women he had loved. No, not loved, she amended cynically, simply wanted. Some impulse she couldn't name made her ask tersely, 'Simon, have you ever loved anyone . . . really loved them I mean?'

The dark eyebrows rose, his mouth twisting again. 'Why? Are you using me as a Father Confessor, Christy . . . wanting to compare emotions and experiences, so that you can tell yourself that what you feel for Miles is the real thing?' His bitterness shocked her.

'Yes, I have loved,' he told her harshly, 'but I doubt that my experience of it matches anything you could feel. Love as I've known it isn't a pleasurable experience, and if you take my advice you'll give it a wide berth.'

His words hit her like blows, devastating her, completely overturning all she had thought she knew about him. There was no doubt that he spoke from the heart, even she could recognise the bitter sincerity of what he was saying, but Simon in love ... loving a woman who to her was a complete stranger ... she wanted to know more. To demand to know the name of this woman who was foolish enough to turn down the rare gift of his caring, but the words simply would not come. She was too raw with pain to voice them. All she wanted to do was to escape from the over-heated tension of the small enclosed space that held them. Simon in love ... having loved and known the pain of that emotion. She could only feel relief when she felt him move away from her and then heard the brief slam of his cabin door.

When she finally brought herself to move she was shaking so badly she could not contain it. Pain washed over her in sheeting waves, almost destroying her. Simon loved someone else ... Until that moment, until he had made that revelation, she had not known how hard she had been clinging to the frail hope that by some miracle he might actually care for her. Now that fragile support was gone and she felt as though she were lost, drowning in a vast boiling sea of agony from which there was no chance of escape or rescue.

CHAPTER SEVEN

AT first when she woke up Christy couldn't imagine what had disturbed her, and then she remembered her dream and struggled to sit up. *Stormsurf* rocked gently in the early morning calm sea and sky, both a soft pale blue as she looked out through her cabin porthole.

She had been dreaming about Kit Masterson and his vessel . . . She had dreamed that she had been on board on that fateful voyage . . . she had heard his voice calling to his men above the lash of the storm, harrying them, willing them, into helping him to save his ship until at last he had had to admit defeat and command them to abandon the vessel.

Even now, fully awake she shuddered, still gripped in the aftershadow of her dream-fear; still able to taste salt on her lips and to hear the vicious scream of the wind . . . It wasn't the first time she had experienced such a vivid dream, but it was the first time she had ever been so involved in an author's work that she had actually dreamed herself into the fabric of his story.

She glanced at her watch. Still not six o'clock, and yet she knew she would never get back to sleep. Somewhere below them lay the *Golden Fleece*, or what was left of her, and as she closed her eyes she re-lived again that dream moment when the waves crashed down over the deck; the sickening crunch of wood against coral; the *Fleece* sinking fast, her hold flooding. Shivering, Christy got up and showered, a sudden tense excitement gripping her. Without being able to analyse why she knew that today they would find something that would prove that that coral-encrusted outline was the *Fleece*. She had to dive ... she couldn't wait for Simon to wake up.

Even knowing that she was disobeying everything he had said didn't stop her from donning her wet-suit. Mechanically she went through the double pack on to her back and then going through the familiar pre-dive rituals. The sea was still calm, almost ominously so, but she put to the back of her mind all Simon's concern about adverse currents. The sea closed over her, enveloping her as she sank slowly downwards. She found the coral outline without too much difficulty, slowly swimming along its length, not knowing what she was looking for but impelled by some instinct so powerful that she had no thought of denying it. Tiny fish darted in panic past her and once she saw the dark shadow of something much larger, but she felt no fear; the compulsion driving her was too strong to admit it.

Time ceased to exist; there was only the coral and this driving urgency that possessed her. And then she stopped, her attention caught by something ... a darker patch on the uniformity of the coral. She swam up to it, her heart thudding slowly in tense excitement as she saw the narrow fissure. It could be anything ... anything at all ... she could be completely wrong in believing that the coral masked the hull of the *Golden Fleece* but something carried her onward, urging her to investigate the narrow aperture.

Normally she would not have contemplated involving herself in such danger, but today things were different. Her slim body only just fitted through the gap and she felt the drag of the sharp coral against her wet-suit as she manoeuvred her upper body with its burden of air tanks through the small space.

Once she was through, her excitement grew. This was no mere gap in a coral wall, but a totally enclosed space; almost totally without light, other than that which seeped in through the opening. Could she be in what had once been the hold of the *Fleece*? Christy was convinced of it, just as she was convinced that somehow there was a link between her dream and her discovery of the opening. Perhaps it was merely a complicated working of her subconscious; perhaps part of her brain had registered the aperture the previous day without her being conscious of it, and then during the night her dream had been the trigger to release that knowledge into her conscious mind; she did not know. Excitement gripped her, possessing her to the exclusion of everything else. If only Simon were down here with her. He was more knowledgeable than her ... he would know what to look for ... She wished she had brought some means of illumination. Now that she had swum a few yards she couldn't see a thing, everything was so dark. Something brushed against her skin and she recoiled, chiding herself. It was probably no more than a frond of seaweed, but in this eerie darkness the sensation of being touched by something unseen was not a pleasant one. Exhilaration gave way to fear, and suddenly she longed for sunlight and air. She felt stifled; breathless almost and it was several seconds before she realised why. She was almost out of air. Quickly she switched to her second tank, cursing herself for not being more careful, but it was impossible to believe that she had been underwater for so long. She must go back and tell Simon what she had found.

She turned round, relieved to see the pinprick of light ahead of her that denoted the opening she had swum through, and for the first time as she swam towards it she acknowledged how foolhardy she had been in coming here alone. Something brushed her arm, and she pushed it away, panic coiling and exploding inside her as, instead of being free, she suddenly found her arm was trapped. In the thin light from the aperture she saw the writhing shape that held her captive and terror froze her as she realised she was imprisoned in the snake-like embrace of a large octopus.

Later she realised that it was her very panic that saved her. The octopus, thinking it had immobilised its prey, momentarily released the tentacle it had wrapped round her arm, and as though someone had pressed a panic button inside her, Christy swam desperately for the opening and its life-giving light. With every stroke she fully expected to feel the unbreakable grip of a tentacle, but it never came. Fresh panic seized her when it seemed she wasn't going to get through the opening; narrower on this side than it was on the other, and at last desperate with fear she reached blindly for the harness securing her oxygen tanks, tearing it off, and praying that she would not destroy the mechanism, as she eased first herself, and then the tanks out into the open sea. The relief she felt then was something she would never forget. It made her tremble from head to foot, so weak that it took her precious minutes to put back her tanks.

When she did she was horrified to discover how

little air she had left. Telling herself she must not panic she swam back along the coral wall, now becoming familiar enough for her to be able to pinpoint the place where she should go to the surface. The desire to get there as fast as she possibly could was something she had to fight, forcing herself to take things slowly and professionally, and when at last she broke the surface and saw the *Stormsurf* rocking easily at anchor less than fifty yards away her relief was so great that she felt weak with it.

She was within feet of the ketch when she saw Simon, and her heart turned over uncomfortably as she saw the uncompromising anger on his face. There was no gentleness in the way he hauled her on board, only savage fury banked down in his eyes as he took the tanks from her, and registered how little air she had left.

'I've found a way inside the coral wall.' How tired and far away her voice sounded; and suddenly she felt almost weak with exhaustion, but if she had expected Simon to praise her she was disappointed.

In a clipped voice he bit out harshly. 'You've gone against every thing I told you before we came out here. You dived without telling me you were going. You took no safety line . . . you stayed down well over one hour.' His control snapped and he reached for her, shaking her until she felt her legs could no longer support her. 'Just what the hell do you think you're doing? This isn't a game, Christy . . .'

She wanted badly to cry . . . so badly that she used up her last reserves of energy in breaking the hold he had on her and stumbling along the deck, down the companionway to her cabin.

Once inside she sank down on her bunk, giving way

to the shudders of reaction coursing through her, knowing that her tears sprang more from the release of fear than Simon's angry words. After all he had every right to be angry. She tugged off her wet-suit, and was just reaching for her robe when the door to her cabin crashed open and Simon stood framed in the doorway, his eyes skimming briefly over her nude body before they settled grimly on her face.

'I hadn't finished.' His voice was implacable, warning her of the anger he was only just holding under control.

Desperate to change the subject Christy said wildly. 'Do you normally walk into women's rooms uninvited?'

For a moment rage flared in his eyes and then he said softly, 'I don't normally need to. They're all too keen to come into mine.'

It was an unkind reminder of her own behaviour at eighteen and her skin took colour from it, her eyes filling with pain.

'Just what the hell were you thinking about?' Simon demanded savagely. Don't you *know* the risks you just ran in running out of air alone ... never mind anything else?' He saw her shiver, not knowing that she was thinking of the octopus, and casually picked up and tossed her her robe. 'Here, put that on.'

She did so quickly, half surprised to realise how unembarrassed she had been by her nudity ... but not as unembarrassed as Simon had been unaroused, she told herself bitterly.

'What made you do it?'

Haltingly she told him about her dream, and the strange conviction that had followed it, expecting with

every breath to hear him making some derisory
comment, but instead he merely expelled a weary
breath, and said quietly, 'You could have wakened me.
Dear God, Christy, have you any idea what I went
through when I came in here to wake you up and
found you missing? You could have fallen overboard,
anything. I was so sure you would never do anything
as foolhardy as diving alone, that it was half an hour
before I thought to check the gear. I didn't even know
where to begin to start looking for you. A hundred
things could have gone wrong. You know that. You
know that solo diving is the most dangerous of all.
Why the hell do you think I was so insistent on us
both wearing safety lines?' She watched him push a
weary hand through his hair, surprised to see how
tired and strained he looked. Of course he probably
felt some sort of responsibility for her ... She might
not be the woman he loved but he was a responsible
human being; she had to acknowledge that.

Six years ago she had been his for the taking, and he
had wanted her, she was sure of that ... but he had
held back; denied himself because he knew he was not
prepared to give her what she wanted. He was more
than a responsible man, she thought tiredly, he was an
honourable one ... She wished she had not made that
discovery; she wished she could find some flaw in him
that would make it less easy for her to love him. What
was she like, this woman he had loved ... and
probably still did love? And why did she not return his
feelings? Perhaps she was already married ...

'Now what are you thinking about?'

Christy looked up at him uncomprehendingly,
noting the rawly strained note in his voice. 'Your eyes

have gone dark grey,' he told her, suddenly reaching out to cup her chin, 'they only do that when you're upset or worried . . .'

'I expect it's shock.' She managed to make her voice sound convincingly light, shivering a little as she tried to move away and for a few seconds it seemed as though he would not release her.

'Have a hot shower, and I'll go and make you a drink. You'll feel better after a few hours sleep.'

'I don't want anything to drink.' She turned away from him, not wanting him to see the weakness in her eyes. She didn't know how long she could endure his presence in the intimate confines of her cabin without throwing herself into his arms and clinging to him for comfort. Every time she closed her eyes she could see the octopus and feel her own fear . . . taste it almost in her mouth.

'Very well.' His mouth compressed and she had the feeling that somehow she had angered him.

Her shower was comforting but nothing like as comforting as the secure strength of Simon's arms would have been, she acknowledged as she climbed into bed. She fell asleep almost instantly, her body and mind both exhausted.

She dreamed about the octopus; horrible, tormented dreams where she writhed helplessly in its tentacles, calling for Simon. But it wasn't the sound of her own screams that eventually woke her and brought her torment to an end, it was Simon shaking her awake, his face anxious and oddly pale as he stared grimly into her sleep-hazed eyes.

'What the devil's going on?' he demanded harshly. 'You were shouting loud enough to raise the devil.'

'A bad dream,' she told him briefly, dragging her eyes away from the sight of his bare torso only inches away from her hand. He was sitting on the edge of her bed, lean fingers loosely grasping her shoulder, the taut muscles of his thighs tense as he leaned towards her.

She waited for him to go, tension holding her body in a painful vice; wanting him to leave and yet not wanting him to do so, her face averted from his, so that when he grasped her shoulders urgently and half lifted and half pulled her back against him, she was too surprised to struggle.

'Come here.' His voice was surprisingly gruff. 'You're all tense.' Her lower back was resting against his thigh, his fingers skilled and supple as he massaged the tight tension between her shoulder blades, finding the pressure points and slowly releasing them, so slowly that she was barely aware of relaxing against him; only of the delicious flow of warmth from his fingers to her skin and the corresponding sense of well being driving out fear and dread. At first when she felt the light warmth of his mouth against her skin she thought she must have imagined it; conjured up that tantalising sensation of delicate exploration because her senses craved it so much, but when it happened again she knew that she had not. Instantly her body tensed, but Simon's hands gripped her upper arms, his voice raw and husky as he muttered, 'Don't stop me Christy . . . don't stop me, we both need this,' and then he was turning her in his arms, pushing her down against the bed and sliding the straps of her nightdress down off her shoulders, slowly revealing the twin curves of her breasts. Outside waves lapped soothingly against the sides of the ketch, the slow rocking motion of the boat lullingly sensuous. Almost as though it were a dream Christy raised her arms, clasping them behind Simon's head, her mouth parting softly in anticipation of the possession of his.

His kissed her slowly, lingeringly, as though his mouth took pleasure merely from the sensation of tasting the softness of hers. Her breath sighed out of her, her body melting, yielding, as Simon pushed away her cotton nightdress and slowly caressed her, his hands cupping her breasts, smoothing across her rib cage, shaping her narrow waist and then the full curve of her hips; the smooth femininity of her thigh.

Desire flamed tinglingly to life inside her, her mouth clinging yearningly to his. It was like floating slowly down to the bottom of the sea; washed by the seductive warmth of sun-warmed water. Simon lifted his mouth from hers, and her fingers burrowed protestingly into his hair, her body arching ... pleading. His tongue traced the moist outline of her lips slipping slowly between them, touching, tasting, until she was wild with the need for more than the gentle seduction of his mouth against her own. Her fingers curled into the smooth muscles of his back, her breasts swelling, her stomach aching as she arched her body into his.

She caught his indecipherable mutter and thrilled to the ring of raw need in it, smothering soft sounds of pleasure into his skin as he released her mouth to trail hot, biting kisses along her throat.

Her hands stroked feverishly over him, unable to absorb enough contact with his skin to satisfy her. She touched her mouth tentatively to his flesh, stunned to discover how hot it was, almost burningly so, but when she made to lift her head, Simon's hand entwined in her hair, holding her locked against him, his voice hoarsely unfamiliar, as he muttered in her ear. 'Yes ... yes. Christy ... kiss me ... God you can't know how my body has ached for the sweet touch of your mouth and your hands.'

His words seemed to release something deep inside her, setting it free; setting *her* free to touch and kiss, to tease him with lightly delicate kisses against his throat and chest which drew jerky mutters of need and praise from his throat. When her tongue brushed delicately over his nipple, he cried out harshly, surprising her, her body wantonly aware of the arousal of his and eager to be closer to the maleness of it. When he moved away from her her body ached with anguish and rejection and as though he read her feelings in her eyes, Christy heard him curse and then say her name thickly as he tore off his shorts and then took her back in his arms, pressing her urgently along the length of his body, muttering soft words into her skin as he soothed it with hot kisses. The touch of his mouth against her breast made her shudder with pleasure and cry out his name, wantonly arching in supplication which he rewarded with slow sucking caresses that destroyed her self-control and left her clinging helplessly to him, until he took her hands and placed them against his body, inciting her to touch and caress him until his own breathing was harsh with pleasure.

A sudden loud bang from the deck startled them both, Christy freezing beneath his caress, Simon's muttered, 'Hell what was that?' tense with male frustration. Almost immediately Christy became aware that the ketch was no longer moving as gracefully; that in fact they were being buffeted much more strongly by the current. In a daze she felt Simon move away from her. 'I'll have to go topside and check what's going on. The wind's changed; I can feel it in the current. Hell and damnation,' he swore, sitting up and reaching for his shorts. 'I wanted to get in another dive before the weather broke.' Gone was the aroused lover, and in his place was the writer, angry because the proof for his novel looked like eluding him.

'I'll get dressed and come up too,' Christy told him when he stood up and opened the door. 'You might need some help.'

It was a good ten minutes before Christy felt able to follow him; ten minutes during which she had once again to acknowledge that she had been saved from revealing to Simon the truth, not by her own caution but by events outside her control. What control? she asked herself bitterly. She seemed to have precious little of that commodity when Simon was around. And what of Simon himself? Sooner or later he was going to expect to take their lovemaking to its natural conclusion. He would not understand any refusal ... How could he when she had just made it more than obvious that she wanted him? Unlike her he apparently did not need to feel love to experience desire. She already knew that he loved someone else, but that did not stop him from desiring her. Her hands shaking, Christy went topside. Simon was engrossed in listening to the radio, and sensing his concentration she did not speak. After a few minutes he turned to her and said briefly, 'The weather's on the change. I thought it might be. With a bit of luck I could get in just one more dive. Now tell me carefully exactly where this aperture is?'

Christy did so, but added dully, 'But it's no use, you won't be able to get inside. It's very narrow, I had to take off my tanks to get out again.'

'Damn.'

She could sense his disappointment, touch it almost.

'I could go down again.' She made the offer tentatively, trying to control her own shudder of fear. Dear God, could she find the courage?

Simon seemed about to refuse and then he said decisively, 'We'll both go down. It's taking a risk to leave the boat, but I'm not prepared to let you go down there alone again.'

They prepared for the dive in silence, Christy leading the way once they had found the coral wall. This time, without the adrenalin of excitement pumping through her veins the opening looked impossibly small. Simon looked at it for several seconds and Christy wondered what he was thinking.

Before they had dived he had told her what he wanted her to do. He wanted her to scour the sea bed and hand out to him any small objects she could find, be they sand-and coral-encrusted or not. He was hoping, she knew, that somehow they might be lucky enough to find some artefact that would prove that they had indeed found the *Golden Fleece*, and as she manoeuvred herself through the opening Christy prayed that she would be successful.

It was a long slow business; the sea bed was several feet below the opening and it was tiring constantly diving down into the darkness, using the small light Simon had given her to search diligently for something small enough to take back to him. She found several indistinguishable lumps of coral and sand, dutifully carrying them back, wondering all the time if ultimately they would prove to be of any benefit. On her third return journey Simon tapped his watch and showed it to her. They had already been down just over an hour. She held up one finger to indicate to him that she would make one more journey and he nodded his head.

This time the fear that she had kept at bay on the other journey's overwhelmed her. What if she should meet another octopus? They liked dark deep places such as this. Simon would not be able to help her. He could not get inside the aperture. Fear shuddered over her, and she fought against it, telling herself that the most dangerous thing she could do was to panic, but all the time she was searching the sea bottom she was tense, constantly looking over her shoulder, haunted by the memory of that dark, sucker-covered tentacle.

She desperately wanted to go back, but as yet she had seen nothing she could possibly carry, and then, just as she was on the point of desperation she saw it, half protruding from the sand, the quite unmistakable handle of some sort of jar, easily recognisable in spite of its covering of weed. She grasped it gently, terrified that it might break and that she would have to start looking all over again, relieved too that she would soon be able to go back to Simon and safety to realise the import of what she had discovered. To her surprise it lifted quite easily, sand spilling from it. It was quite large, and amazingly appeared to be completely intact, not a jug as she had first thought but some sort of drinking vessel. Holding it carefully she swam quickly back. Simon was waiting for her, and she handed him her trophy, sensing his stunned surprise, as he placed it carefully in the rope basket with the other things she had brought. Then he was helping her through the aperture, holding her tanks as she took them off, quickly strapping them back on for her once she herself was through and then swiftly guiding her back along the wall, monitoring their climb upwards, helping her towards and into the ketch as her tired body threatened to give way to the insidious pull of the slowly increasing current. Now, standing shivering on board the ketch she could see only too easily all the many unpleasant fates that could have overtaken her that morning. The current had greatly increased, the sea boiling ominously over the coral. She shivered again and Simon ordered peremptorily, 'Go below and shower, you look frozen.'

'What about you?' She hesitated, missing the closeness they had shared earlier, and yet knowing that it would be wise to preserve a distance between them.

'I'm okay. I'll come down later, once we're out of these waters. There's a storm blowing up.'

Christy looked at the sky, which still looked placidly blue, and yet there was a slight brassiness to the golden haze of the sun; a tension in the air which didn't spring entirely from her own inner turmoil.

By the time she had showered and dressed, the promontory was slowly fading behind them. Simon left her in charge of the wheel while he went down to shower and change and when he came back up Christy went below to make them both a meal. It was while they were eating it that he made his first reference to her finds.

'I have no idea what we've got. The drinking vessel looks interesting and God knows what's buried beneath those lumps of coral. I think the best thing to do is for us to return to England—we can have them properly examined there, and while we're waiting for the results I can start work.'

'But I thought you wanted to write your book here,' Christy protested, a sudden spasm of intuition telling her that it was in some way because of her; because he no longer wanted to be so dangerously alone with her that he was suggesting this course. So much for her earlier belief that he intended to make love to her! It was no real surprise to discover that she felt pain and disappointment instead of relief.

'I did, but I've changed my mind.'

'Then once we get back you won't be needing me any more,' she managed to say quite casually.

'I engaged you to work for me until the book's completed.' His voice was unusually harsh. 'What's the matter? Afraid Miles might not approve?'

She had almost forgotten that he believed her to have been involved with Miles and she blushed guiltily, wondering what interpretation he had put on her feverish response to *his* lovemaking. Did he think she was promiscuous, or perhaps simply suffering from sexual frustration? Neither thought was particularly flattering, but surely infinitely preferable to him discovering the truth, she reminded herself wryly. Surely *anything* was preferable to that now that she knew there was no hope of him ever returning her love?

CHAPTER EIGHT

THEY flew into Heathrow from St Lucia almost twenty-four hours later. The items Christy had retrieved from the sea bed had been packed in a crate and were on board the 707 with them as were all Simon's papers and notes relating to Kit Masterson.

She had half expected him to suggest that she return home to the vicarage, but he seemed determined to hold her to their original contract. There was plenty of room for both of them in his Knightsbridge apartment he told her, adding cynically that there was also the presence of his housekeeper if she was concerned about the moral ethics of sharing the apartment with him.

They drove there in silence from the airport, Christy because she was too tired after the long flight to make polite conversation and Simon because he seemed to be engrossed in deep thoughts of his own.

In order to while away the journey Christy had tried to do some more drawings of Kit Masterson, but to her chagrin the only face that would take shape beneath her pencil was Simon's. Not even the addition of a dashing Elizabethan beard and an ornate gold earring in one ear had been able to destroy that likeness, and in the end she had had to crumple up what she had done and dispose of it in her handbag. Now they were back in London—far sooner than she had expected. Did the woman Simon loved live here— was that one of the reasons for their precipitous departure? It was a thought that hadn't occurred to her before but now that it had, her whole body ached bitterly with jealousy and pain. Who was she? She could, of course, always ask Simon, but she doubted that he would answer her. Why should he? She thought of what he had told her about his early life, and how for a brief span of time she had thought that perhaps he was telling her because he wanted them to be closer but all he had ever wanted from her was the fleeting satisfaction of making love to her—nothing more. And now it seemed that even that desire had gone to judge from the speed with which he had whisked them both back to England. And yet he had spoken derisively about moral ethics. *Her* moral ethics and the chaperonage of his housekeeper, or had that merely been a subtle warning? After all she had made no attempt to reject his advances, despite the fact that she had not refuted his suggestions that she and Miles were involved in some sort of relationship. Too tired to sort order from her muddled thoughts Christy closed her eyes and let the familiar sounds of the London traffic well over her. When she opened them again everything was silent.

'We're here,' Simon told her unnecessarily, as he shook her awake. 'Here' was obviously the underground carpark to his apartment, and Christy was glad of the lack of proper daylight to hide her flushed confusion from him. How could she have fallen asleep, and leaning on Simon's shoulder too, to judge from the angle at which she was sitting.

'I'll take the bags,' Simon told her, unlocking the boot. 'Come on,' he added once he had got them, 'it's this way.'

A lift bore them upwards, the atmosphere inside it thick with tension and a certain amount of hostility. Gone was the man she had come to want as a friend and lover while they had been in the Caribbean. This man who stood in his place was the one she had shrunk from and loathed the thought of seeing again the summer she was eighteen and during the intervening six years. Perhaps it was England that had that effect on him, Christy thought acidly, as the lift stopped and Simon gestured to her to precede him. Or perhaps it was just her. It hurt to think that someone else had shared that softer, almost tender side of him while she had been shown the cold face of his hostile indifference.

They were in a small bare foyer. Simon put down their bags and unearthed a key from his pocket, fitting it in the lock.

'The front entrance operates on a security system,' he told her briefly as they walked inside. 'Later I'll familiarise you with it.' He looked at his watch. It was just gone ten o'clock in the morning and they had been travelling most of the night. Waves of weariness beat down on Christy. All she really wanted to do was to go to sleep.

'This way.'

Christy followed Simon from the hall into a large elegantly furnished drawing room. The apartment must be huge, she reflected studying the acres of impossibly pale cream carpet and the smooth masculinity of the matching leather furniture. Paintings on the walls provided the odd touch of colour, together with several silk cushions and the heavy, rich velvet curtains. A man's room, uncluttered without being too cold.

'Dining room,' Simon intoned, opening another door so that she had a brief glimpse of a startlingly Oriental room in rich reds and black. 'Kitchen's on the other side of it—you'll find that's mainly Mrs Pargetter's domain. She must be out shopping now. I telephoned to warn her to expect us.' He indicated another door and pushed it open so that she could see the book-shelf lined walls and the huge desk. 'My study . . . that's where we'll be working. Unfortunately large though the apartment is it doesn't enable me to provide you with your own room.'

He took her back across the drawing room and opened another door into an inner hallway. 'Two bedrooms,' he told her, 'each with its own bathroom. Mrs Pargetter's is on the other side of the kitchen, together with her sitting room. This room's mine.' He indicated the first door without opening it, 'and this one will be yours.' He pushed open the door and Christy followed him inside. The room was large, the double bed surrounded by elegant fitted furniture. The colour scheme was predominantly peach without being over-feminine. 'Bathroom over there,' Simon told her indicating yet another door. 'I'll bring in your bags and then leave you to get settled. If you feel like having a sleep by all means do so, I shan't need you now until tomorrow.'

'And you?' Christy questioned, suddenly paralysingly shy. Here, back in London he was like a different man almost. 'Will you sleep?'

His expression was sardonic. 'I doubt it. You forget I'm more used to the long flight than you. I find it difficult to sleep during the day anyway. I've got some

notes I want to work on—there'll be post to catch up
on, and then I want to check that the crate's delivered
properly. So you see,' his voice was tautly mocking,
'you need not fear that I'm likely to disturb your
chaste slumbers. I'll be far too busy.'

Her cheeks stung at the deliberate cruelty of the jibe
and Christy turned her face away. 'It never occurred
to me that you might,' she said with quiet dignity,
unaware of his quick frown, or the way he moved
fractionally towards her, only to draw back.

'I'll leave you to sleep then.'

'Your apartment is very pleasant.' Heavens how
stilted she sounded and yet she was so reluctant for
him to go away; even to the extent of making polite
conversation simply to keep him there. If only life
could be more simple; if she could just say to him, 'I
love you and I want you to stay with me. I want to go
to sleep in your arms, my body satiated by your
lovemaking,' but of course to say anything of the kind
was completely impossible.

'I bought it from the previous owner with
everything included. He was an interior designer.' He
pulled a wry face. 'Some of the decor—in the dining
room for instance—is not exactly to my taste, but as a
temporary abode it isn't too bad.'

Temporary? Christy's heart started to knock heavily
against her ribs. Was he planning to leave Britain
then? Live in America perhaps. Or make his home on
St Paul's? She could hardly ask him, and it was an
indication of the intensity of her feelings that she
should experience such a deep sensation of loss simply
at the thought of him living in another country.

Fool she derided herself as he left and she wandered

into her luxuriously appointed bathroom. Tired
though she was she could not go to bed without first
showering away the grime of the journey.

She showered apathetically, the warm sting of the
water doing nothing to revive her, and it was only as
she was drying herself that she remembered that she
had nothing to wear. Shrugging she wrapped herself
in a dry towel. She would find a nightdress when
Simon brought her bags, for now she felt so tired that
all she wanted to do was to lie down.

She walked into the bedroom and discovered that
her cases were already there, but it was too much of an
effort to bother opening them. Without even stopping
to pull back the covers she lay face down on the bed
still wrapped in the protective towel, knowing that she
would be asleep within seconds.

She didn't even hear the door open and was
completely oblivious to Simon's presence as he
hesitated beside her, a mug of coffee in one hand and a
deep frown creasing his forehead as he stared down at
her. At last with an almost angry sigh, he unwrapped
the damp towel from her body, pulling down the
bedclothes and gently easing her beneath them. She
moved only once, when his hand accidentally grazed
the side of her breast, a half smile parting her lips, a
small sound of pleasure murmuring from them.
Slowly Simon straightened up and stared down at her,
his frown deeper, a derisive smile twisting his lips as
he studied her for a moment before turning and
walking out.

When Christy awoke it was late afternoon. She
stretched indolently, tensing when she suddenly
realised that she was naked and that moreover she was

lying beneath the sheets when before she had been lying on top. Who had put her there, not Mrs Pargetter surely? Her skin flushed at the thought of Simon seeing and touching her, and yet it was not resentment or anger that brought the soft colour up under her flesh.

Up and dressed she wandered aimlessly round the apartment for half an hour before deciding to go out. Pulling on a jacket she hurried down to the main foyer, explaining to the commissionaire who she was.

'That's all right, Miss,' he told her reassuringly. 'Mr Jardine's already told me about you.'

Once outside she shivered slightly in the cool June breeze. London felt unmistakably chilly after the Caribbean. She would need some warmer clothes if she was to stay here for very long. Which reminded her that she would have to 'phone her mother. Knightsbridge itself was busy, thronged with shoppers and tourists, but she managed to find a small bookshop where she was able to purchase a couple of magazines and a light novel to read.

She had no idea what time Simon would return, or indeed how she would be expected to spend the evening. Simon could well have a date. A knife-sharp pain twisted her heart, but it was something she had to force herself to face, she decided as she re-traced her steps in the direction of his apartment.

'Christy!'

For a moment the sound of her own name startled her. She stopped and looked round, a smile breaking out across her face as she recognised Miles hurrying towards her.

'Christy . . . what on earth are you doing here? Your

mother told me you were in the Caribbean working for Simon Jardine.'

'I was . . . I am . . .' Christy responded breathlessly, returning his briefly casual kiss. 'That is I am working for Simon and we were in the Caribbean but now we're back.'

'So I see. I've just driven your mother to the airport.'

When he saw her surprise he told her, 'Jeremy persuaded her to go with him to America to talk about a new deal for her books. Look, what are you doing tonight?' he asked her. 'Can you manage dinner?'

'Well, I don't know. . . . I'm not sure what Simon's got planned—if he wants me to work,' she amended. 'He's out at the moment and as I was at a loose end I decided to come out and get myself something to read. How are you?' she asked belatedly, 'I hear your book's doing very well.'

'No little thanks to my extremely able assistant,' Miles agreed with a wry smile. 'I'm fine—if somewhat disillusioned by the side-effects of fame.'

Christy's eyebrows rose, as she sensed the tension in him. 'Problems?' she enquired.

'Of a kind. While I was on tour in Germany I became very friendly with a man I met over there—a very powerful personality in the German publishing field. The only problem is he's got a daughter and said daughter seems to believe she's fallen in love with me.' Miles smile was extremely wry. 'She's barely nineteen and extremely persistent. She and her father are in London at the moment. I was supposed to be taking them out to dine tonight, but Daddy has cried off at the last minute and it seems that she and I are to dine *a deux* . . .'

'Oh dear, poor you.' Laughter sprang readily to Christy's eyes, although she felt a small tug of sympathy for the German girl. She too knew what it was to fall madly in love with a man who was totally uninterested . . . Although that wasn't completely true. Simon had been interested in her, if only in a purely sexual way.

'I'd give anything to get out of it, but Jeremy is adamant that I mustn't offend Daddy. When I saw you I was hoping you might be my salvation and that I could persuade you to join us.'

'As what?' Christy asked him bluntly.

'As protection.' He was equally honest. 'Imogen's a nice enough girl but I'm not in the market for marriage, Christy. Not now . . . not ever perhaps.' His expression was faintly defensive as he added. 'You know how it is with me. Sex isn't and never has been a driving force in my life. You must have guessed that when we were in India?'

Christy had, and she had been relieved to discover it, knowing that there would be no unwanted complications such as having to fend off his advances and risk offending him in doing so. They were good friends; she knew that Miles preferred the company of older women, and although they had never spoken of it she guessed he had a slightly ambivalent feeling towards her sex. However, that was his private affair, and she liked him enough to feel sorry for him because his almost too-perfect blond good looks were bound to draw her sex to him, and she guessed that as he grew more famous Imogen would not be the only female he would have to fight off.

'When I saw you, I thought you could be the answer to all my prayers,' he added with a grimace.

'You mean a shield to use against Imogen? The faithful "girlfriend" perhaps?'

'You've guessed it,' he admitted. 'I know we never discussed it when we were in India, but then there didn't seem to be anyone particular in your life. If there still isn't and if you could help me, I'd be extremely grateful to you, Christy.'

What if she agreed? It would help both of them. Simon already seemed to believe there was some sort of romantic attachment between them; if she agreed to pose as Miles' 'girlfriend' she could reinforce that view. She doubted somehow that now they were back in London Simon would make any attempt to make love to her; she was safe enough from that point of view, but what about her own feelings; her own helpless sensation of needing to reach out and touch him? Could *she* control that? Wouldn't giving herself the official status of being Miles' girlfriend help her to keep her own feelings under control?

'Christy?'

She pushed aside her thoughts and smiled into Miles' anxious blue eyes. 'Yes, of course I'll help you,' she told him. Who knew? she might even be doing Imogen a favour in preventing the younger girl from falling too deeply in love with Miles before it was too late.

'And you'll join us for dinner tonight?'

How could she refuse? Simon had said he wouldn't want to start work until the morning. She could hardly see him objecting.

'Yes.'

They arranged that Miles would pick her up from Simon's apartment at eight, and then as she realised that she had nothing with her that was suitable to wear to go out to dinner, she excused herself, telling him that she would have to do some shopping.

She could hardly be living anywhere more convenient, or tempting, she reflected half an hour later, studying her reflection in the mirror as she tried on a particularly sensational Valentino outfit.

The rich blue silk shimmered seductively against her skin, the sleek outline of the dress hugging her slender figure, outlining the curves of her breasts and thighs. Buttons fastened the dress from top to bottom, tiny shoestring straps showing off her golden tan. A matching jacket went with it, and closing her mind against its extortionate price she produced her credit card, reflecting that it was just as well that Simon was paying her a good salary.

Shoes came next, and then some make-up since she had not taken more than the basic necessities to the Caribbean with her. Although supposedly all this expense was for the benefit of Miles and Imogen a tiny voice inside her whispered that it was Simon she wanted to see her dressed in the rich blue silk, looking remarkably like the wildly passionate gypsy girl he had once, derisively, called her.

The apartment was empty when she got back but she found a note in the kitchen from Mrs Pargetter saying that she had had to go to Kew to see her sister, who had apparently suffered a bad fall. 'Fridge and freezer stocked,' Christy read. 'Back as soon as possible!'

She took her time getting ready, ears straining for

the sound of Simon's return, not wanting to admit her
own disappointment when she was eventually ready
and he had not come back. The dress looked more
revealing in the privacy of her room than it had done
in the shop. It also seemed to mould her body far
more seductively than she had remembered, the rich
blue fabric clinging to her body with every small
movement she made. She had used slightly more
theatrical make-up than usual—dark eyeshadow which
brought into prominence the slanting wantonness of
her eyes, blusher frosting her high cheekbones and her
full mouth warmly pink.

The satin shoes she had found in Rayne's were an
excellent match for her dress, and as she sprayed
herself lightly with the *Joy* which she had bought as a
duty-free present from her mother, she wondered if
Imogen would be impressed.

Simon had still not returned when Miles came to
pick her up, his eyes widening fractionally as he
studied her. She could sense his shock and wondered
if she had gone a little over the top.

'You look ... stunning,' he said at length, 'I've
never seen you looking like this before.'

Come to think of neither had she, Christy reflected,
studying her reflection for a moment in the full-length
wall mirror in the hallway. Tonight she looked every
inch the wild gypsy girl Simon had once called her;
even her eyes seemed to gleam with dangerous
wantonness, her mouth provocatively full, her body
slimly supple in its sheath of blue silk, unexpectedly
unfamiliar to her, just as her whole reflection gave
back the image of a woman with whom she was
unfamiliar. She looked quite different and the

knowledge shocked her, almost as though she had
come face to face with a part of herself from which she
had previously hidden.

They were a little late arriving at the hotel where
Imogen and her father were staying. Miss von Trecht
was waiting for them in the cocktail bar, a uniformed
waiter informed Miles.

All the sympathy Christy had been feeling towards
the younger girl vanished when she came face to face
with her. Only nineteen Imogen von Trecht might be,
but there was no pretension to youth or innocence in
the hard blue eyes and the sulky, over-painted mouth.
The look she gave Christy was insulting in the
extreme, her blonde head tilting towards Miles and
she took his arm in a proprietorial gesture.

'Ah yes,' she said when Miles had introduced them.
'You were Miles' assistant in India, I believe.'

The way she said it made Christy feel as though she
were a duchess talking about the lowest scullery maid,
but she held on to her temper, and remembering her
supposed role stood at the other side of Miles, her
fingertips resting lightly on his arm as she said softly.
'Yes, that's right, isn't it, darling?'

The endearment hung on the air between them, and
in other circumstances Christy would have been
impelled to laugh, so acutely uncomfortable was
Miles' expression, and yet there was no mistaking the
plea in the look he sent her and she responded to it,
smiling at him again, letting her lashes veil her eyes
seductively, pressing her body a little closer to his, as
the waiter came to inform them that their table was
ready.

The von Trecht's were staying at the Connaught,

and although Christy had dined there before, the hotel had a sufficiently impressive reputation for her to feel slightly ill at ease.

She was not surprised when Imogen took the lead, walking at Miles' side towards the table, so that she was forced to bring up the rear. So much for her supposition that Imogen was a vulnerable and perhaps shy teenager. Nothing could have been further from the truth. Imogen was all woman—and a very determined and sophisticated one at that. No wonder Miles had been so worried. Couldn't Imogen see that at heart he was not a deeply sexual man; or was that why she wanted him? The challenge of making him want her? Or did she simply want him because he was a well-known writer? People had married for less, and Miles had told her that he was convinced that it was marriage that Imogen had on her mind. Poor Miles; told by Jeremy not to offend the father, what would he have done if she hadn't been able to come to his rescue?

They were half-way through their first course when Christy became aware of being the object of someone's scrutiny. She couldn't say what made her conscious of being watched, she just knew that she was. She could almost feel the pressure of unseen eyes studying her. It was an uncomfortable sensation and she searched the dining room discreetly, eventually resorting to the ploy of bending down to pick up her handbag so that she could look behind her.

As she did so her eyes clashed immediately with Simon's. He was sitting three tables away, dining with a man who was a complete stranger to her, his mouth carved into a bitterly derisive line as he studied her flushed face. What was Simon doing here?

Why shouldn't he be here? she asked herself. It was a coincidence that he should be of course, but nothing more. You wanted him to see you in all your finery she reminded herself as she turned her attention back to her now unwanted meal. But not like this ... not studying her with all the cool insolence of a man intent on stripping what there was of the blue silk from her body, together with everything she might be wearing underneath. And Simon had no need to use his considerably powerful imagination to furnish himself with mental pictures of her naked body she reminded herself, he already knew exactly what she looked like, right down to the mole that nestled against the inner curve of her right breast. She should know. Without needing the slightest effort of will she could all too vividly remember the sensation of his mouth moving against it, caressing the small birthmark.

'Christy, are you all right?' Miles' voice was concerned, reaching her, it seemed across a vast distance.

'I'm fine.' She wasn't. She could feel perspiration breaking out across her forehead. Her stomach was churning and she felt quite sick. Ridiculous sensations to experience simply because of the way Simon had looked at her, and yet experiencing them she was.

She was here to help Miles, she reminded herself, trying to pull herself together enough to field Imogen's outrageously catty remarks. Had she really been in love with Miles, really his girlfriend, she would not have found the other girl so amusing. Some of her remarks were too obviously designed to hurt to be worthy of attention but others were more subtle, indicating that during his stay in Germany she and

Miles had been more than mere friends. A girlfriend could have been made to feel extremely jealous by what Imogen was saying. If, for instance, it had been Simon sitting where Miles was, she doubted she could have born Imogen's poison tipped remarks with composure, never mind indifference.

'After we've eaten Miles, Daddy would like to see you in his suite,' Imogen informed them over coffee, darting Christy a hostile glance which made it plain that she was excluded from the invitation.

Miles' expression was agonised, imploring Christy to come to his rescue. Out of the corner of her eye she saw Simon rise and realised that he and his companion had finished eating and were coming in their direction. They were almost level with their table when she realised that Miles was still waiting for her to rescue him. Wildly she wondered what on earth she could say, and then her ever-vivid imagination came to her rescue.

'Don't worry, darling.' She deliberately pitched her voice to husky provocativeness. 'I'll go straight home and wait there for you. I'll even make you your favourite nightcap. We can share it together when you get back.' Her eyes and voice promised that they would share more than a mere drink and she could feel the relief flooding through Miles just as she could see Imogen's increasing hostility.

'Yes. You do that, my love, I shouldn't be too long.'

'No.' Christy gave Imogen a cool smile. 'If your father's ill, he won't want to keep Miles for very long.'

Rage flashed in Imogen's eyes, but Christy was beyond feeling sorry for her.

'I'll come and see you into a taxi,' she heard Miles saying at her side, his hand under her elbow as he

guided her out of the restaurant. She was just in time
to see Simon and his companion getting into a taxi . . .
Thank goodness he had gone. She had gone into this
charade with Miles, partly because of Simon, it was
true, but she had found it almost impossible to
maintain her self-imposed role under his derisive eyes.
Had he seen through her play-acting? She shivered
slightly, and Miles was instantly concerned. 'I should
take you back to Simon's apartment,' he told her, 'but
I can't see how I can get out of this meeting. Thanks
for rescuing me by the way . . .'

'Well, let's hope Imogen doesn't go to the extent of
accompanying you back to your house just to check
that I'm actually there waiting for you,' Christy joked.
She knew that Miles owned a small Mews house in
Chelsea because she had visited it when she worked
for him.

'Unlikely. Her father's extremely strict, believe it or
not, and had he been with us tonight you'd have seen a
completely different side of her. Talk about butter
wouldn't melt . . . The first time we were alone I
couldn't believe it; she seemed to turn from little girl
into . . . well what you saw tonight right in front of my
eyes . . . I can't think why she's pursuing me so
determinedly, I should have thought someone like
Simon Jardine was much more her cup of tea.' He
looked so glum that Christy had to laugh.

'Don't worry,' she told him, 'I'll do my best to
protect you from her.'

'I don't suppose I could persuade you to get
engaged to me could I?' Miles asked wistfully. 'Only
on a strictly temporary basis,' he amended hurriedly,
'I think that might put her off completely.'

'It would be rather a drastic step to take,' Christy told him. 'For one thing we couldn't guarantee that it wouldn't get to the ears of the Press ... then there'd be explanations to make to all sorts of people ... my mother for one, and Jeremy for another.'

'Yes, I suppose you're right.'

A taxi arrived and Christy hurried towards it. Poor Miles, she thought sympathetically as she subsided inside it and gave the driver Simon's address.

The commissionaire welcomed her with a smile and let her into the private lift.

She had no key but luckily the door was on the latch and swung open to reveal that the foyer was in darkness. So was the drawing room and it was with a feeling of relief that Christy made her way across it towards the kitchen. Simon it seemed wasn't back. Quite why that should make her feel relieved she wasn't sure, she only knew she was.

Her hand was on the kitchen door when a voice behind her, soft and openly derisive, froze her to the spot.

'Well, well,' Simon drawled softly. 'You're back early. What happened? Didn't he come up to scratch?' He reached out, switching on a lamp, coming to his feet, to tower over her, the lamp throwing his shadow across the room, the shadows cloaking his expression in a way that was almost menacing. His anger was almost tangible, coupled with a savagery she could not understand. He came over to her, moving as lithely and stalkingly as a jungle cat, his fingers flicking open the unbuttoned silk of her jacket and resting just against the edge of her dress, barely touching her skin and yet filling her with an intensely disturbing

emotion. He laughed deep in his throat and it wasn't a
pleasant sound. 'I might have known you'd go running
to him the moment my back was turned. What's he
got that I haven't, Christy? It sure as hell isn't the
ability to satisfy you. Look at yourself.' His fingers
tangled in her hair as he half pulled and half dragged
her into the foyer, snapping on the light so that she
was confronted with her own image in the mirror.
Bruised grey eyes stared back at her, her heart
thumping almost visibly beneath the soft silk. 'Look,'
Simon insisted thickly. 'Look at your eyes . . . your
mouth . . . your body . . . Do you think you look like a
woman who's just found satisfaction in a man's arms?'

'I didn't go to Miles for that.' The denial was
wrenched from her throat, born of a primitive fear she
could not name.

'No?' Simon's laugh was openly bitter. 'Then why
did you dress like this for him?' His fingers pushed
open the silk jacket and revealed her dress. 'Why did
you go to him with your body wrapped in silk so very
provocatively that to look at you is to want you, if it
wasn't because you wanted him to make love to you?'
he demanded harshly.

There was no answer she could give him. Certainly
she could not tell him the truth, which she now knew
to be that she had used Miles as an excuse and that she
had chosen the dress for him . . . that she had wanted
him to see and desire her . . . and nor could she tell
him about Imogen. To do that was to rob herself of
what little protection she had left.

'It's my right to take a lover if I want one.'

Where did those defiant words come from? Christy
could scarcely believe she had voiced them. She saw

the rage glitter deep in Simon's eyes; felt the harsh sound of his indrawn breath, his fingers tightening against her skin as he breathed rawly. 'Then take *me*, Christy. My God,' he snarled bitterly in the silence that followed, 'you owe it to me for all you've put me through.'

'*I've* put *you* through?' She was bitterly incredulous. 'The boot was very much on the other foot as I remember it.'

She watched his mouth twist. 'Was it?'

What was he trying to do to her? 'Was it, Christy?' he muttered thickly pulling her into his arms and holding her, making her aware of his arousal. 'I wanted you six years ago and I want you now,' he told her simply, 'and there was a time, briefly, when we were away when I believed you wanted me. Was I wrong?'

What could she say? Her mind urged her to deny it, but her heart and her body wouldn't allow her to lie.

'No.'

'Then why,' he murmured persuasively, 'should we not be lovers?'

What could she say? That she loved him and he did not love her? That he loved someone else? Would that stop him? She doubted it. He had never been a man to be swayed by emotions. But there was something else ... Her body trembled as she faced him. She would tell him the truth, or at least part of it and then it was up to him; he could reject her or ... or not, as he chose.

'Why?' she managed to step away from him and back into the drawing room, sinking down into a chair as she did so. 'It's quite simple really.' Did she sound as nervous as she felt? 'You see, Simon, I'm afraid that I'm still a virgin.' She didn't look at him. She couldn't. She badly wanted a drink but even had she had one she doubted she could have lifted the glass to her lips without dropping it. 'Had you and I just met, if there had been no past between us, it wouldn't have mattered, but there *was* a past between us, and moreover you did tell me how you felt about virgins ...' she managed a brief shrug ... 'I found that combination somewhat inhibiting to say the least.'

'Why?' The question was snapped at her, and she made no pretence of not understanding. She had come so far; she had to find the courage to go on. 'No real reason; there was simply never anyone who excited me enough for me to want them as my lover.' She attempted a rueful smile which died as he grasped her, hauling her to her feet, his eyes glittering dangerous over her face. 'And me, Christy? Do I excite you enough? Does your body want me as its lover?'

She quivered tensely for a second and then admitted quietly, 'You must know that it does. At long last I've learned that love and desire can exist separately.' She told him that because she didn't want him to guess the truth, but for some reason her remark seemed to displease him. His mouth curled slightly.

'Meaning, I suppose, that you believe yourself in love with Miles.'

She made to pull away from him, but he wouldn't release her. 'Oh no, Christy, you don't escape me like that,' he told her softly. 'You've already admitted that you want me as your lover ... and I want you,' he added. 'Oh yes, I want you.' He picked her up as easily as though she were a child and walked into the inner hall with her, shouldering open the door to his own room.

'But I'm still a virgin.' She was practically gabbling; half frightened and half excited by what she had set in motion.

'In you it's a flaw I'm prepared to overlook. Besides,' he paused beside the bed, without lowering her on to it, 'it's a condition that's easily remedied.'

'Simon.' Panic flared in her voice.

'Be quiet.' He muttered the command thickly against her mouth, imprisoning her against the bed, stopping both her protest and her breath with his kiss.

When he released her he looked down into her face and said slowly. 'When you told me you wanted me you gave yourself into my hands, Christy, whether you're prepared to admit it or not. In telling me you're still a virgin you handed the decisions over to me, so don't argue now about the way I make them.' He reached out and snapped on the bedside light, revealing the dark masculinity of the decor to her. 'Six years I've waited to know you gypsy girl . . .' His voice was slightly slurred, 'and six years is a hell of a long time for a man to go hungry.'

CHAPTER NINE

SHE ought to stop him, Christy knew that but his words had struck an answering chord deep inside her. She too was hungry ... hungry for the scent and touch of him ... for the heat of his body against hers ... for the knowledge that she had the power to arouse him and so appease the need he aroused in her.

His hands shaped her body a little less surely than she had imagined and with a far greater need, his fingers trembling over her dress buttons. His mouth on her throat, her breasts and then against her own mouth hotly feverish, revealing a passion that sent thrills of response shivering over her skin. She had expected to feel slightly gauche; to be burdened by the full weight of her inexperience, but instead there was no room for any feelings other than those engendered by his touch; by knowing that this man who she held in her arms against her body was *the* man, whom she always had, and always would, love. But that was her secret, not to be whispered; not even to be thought while she was here with Simon, lest she betray it to him. He was not seducing her with false promises; he had made no protestations of a love he obviously could not feel, but he did want her; dear God she had not known that mere wanting could be so intense; so all-consuming that it could change a man almost beyond recognition so that he was stripped of his self-control and urbanity revealing a hunger and need that almost made him seem acutely vulnerable.

It should have given her a feeling of power; of knowing that for once she was the one to control the passage of their relationship but instead it made her feel something approaching humility and she wrapped her arms round him protectively, a great tide of emotion rising up and drowning out everything but this moment in time; now when at last they were together.

Eagerly she helped him out of his clothes, both awed and aroused by the sight of his naked body, touching him tentatively and then thrilling to the look in his eyes as he in turn studied her long-limbed body.

He took her hands and placed a kiss in the palms of them both before placing them against his body.

She could feel the faint prickle of his dark chest hair against her skin, the moistness of his flesh beneath her own. His mouth touched hers softly, slowly as though he relished the taste of her. Anticipation quivered through her stomach as he teased her lips with delicate kisses and she slid her arms round his neck, holding him to her, her mouth parting eagerly, enticingly; his name leaving her lips on a soft plea.

'Kiss me, Simon,' she begged him, curling her fingers into his hair, arching her body wantonly against him.

'I thought I was doing.' His voice was thick and slightly slurred, the hands that gripped her waist betraying a tension that belied his teasing words.

'Not like that.'

'Then how. Show me.' He murmured the words against her mouth and her need for him ached through her body. If she couldn't find the words to tell him how much she wanted and needed him, at least she could show him. Her mouth clung passionately to his, her hands moving feverishly over his skin, until he gave a harsh groan, moulding her to the length of his aroused body; taking control of the kiss; taking control of *her*, Christy thought wildly as her body responded eagerly to his barely leashed passion.

'Christy!' The harsh sound of her name exploded into the silence between them, her body trembling in response to the need contained within it. His thighs trapped hers; dark hair-roughened skin against paler more feminine flesh. His hands cupped her breasts, his mouth savouring the throbbing temptation of her nipples, making her arch and move restlessly beneath him, calling out his name; wanting him with a shameless urgency she had no thought of hiding.

His hands gave her a licence to touch his body; learning it slowly, thrilled by the masculinity of it and a little afraid of the hunger her touch seemed to arouse in him and then as his mouth continued to explore her body, her fear of him forgotten in the shock of discovering that what she had thought of as the pinnacle of pleasure when his mouth touched her breasts had simply been the foothills of some far-distant and only now just barely glimpsed peaks.

Her thighs parted willingly to his intimate exploration of her body, the soft stroke of his fingers drawing small shudders of pleasure from her she didn't seek to hide.

She sensed that he was controlling his own need and passion in order to fuel hers; but she didn't want restraint and care; she wanted them to be equal partners in a mutually pleasurable journey of passion and the frantic movement of her body; the hot, impassioned kisses she placed against his skin told him so.

'Simon . . . please . . . I want you so . . .' The words were muffled by the kisses she was scattering against his body, but he still managed to hear them, tensing for a moment and then muttering thickly. 'Hush . . . no . . . not yet,' and then when she moved tormentingly against him, he added hoarsely . . . 'Christy . . . Christy, I don't want to hurt you.'

He didn't want to *hurt* her! She just managed to control an hysterical bubble of bitter laughter. He had already hurt her more than he would ever know simply by loving someone else instead of her; and that hurt would be with her far longer than any mere brief physical pain.

'Simon . . . please . . . please . . .' She arched her body and ground her hips impatiently against his, achingly aware of his arousal, and wanting more, so much more than the fierce tug of his mouth against her breasts and the tormenting stroke of his fingers touching her intimately. Her teeth bit urgently into his shoulder, her hands stroking feverishly along his back and then as he pulled slightly away from her, over his narrow hips and the flat tautness of his stomach; lower still, blindly giving in to her instincts, tracing the dark shadowing of body hair, touching and stroking until he gasped her name in hoarse supplication, his mouth burning fevered kisses against her skin as he kneeled over her, tracing a scorching line of them along a similar path to that she had just followed, with an equally devastating effect on her senses to the one she had had on his.

His mouth touched her inner thigh and she
trembled wildly unsure if she was ready for such
intimacy, but Simon took no heed of her smothered,
half-inarticulate protests, his hands and mouth working
a subtle magic that silenced her protests, changing
them to small cries of pleasure-sheathed urgency.

Waves of sensation beat over her, her body writhing
helplessly beneath his touch; his name a repetitive
gasped prayer on her lips as her body ached to be
completely possessed by his. As he entered her Christy
cried out with pleasure, but Simon, mistaking it for
pain, hesitated, his eyes searching hers, his body tense.
He might not love her, Christy realised, looking at
him, but he thought enough of her to show her every
care; to be concerned for her pleasure above his own.
A wave of love for him swamped her and she arched
beneath him, feeling the tremor that ran through him,
her fingers curling into the smooth muscles of his
back, her lips parting for his kiss as she mouthed
softly, 'Love me, Simon . . . love me now . . . please.'

She felt the controlled thrust of his body and
welcomed its intimate invasion; any pain so brief that
it was swiftly forgotten. She knew the exact moment
Simon's control broke; felt it in the powerful surge of
his body into her own; heard it in the harsh mingled
sound of pleasure and torment that left his throat and
she rejoiced in knowing that now—at last—they met as
equals; joined by a hunger and need neither of them
could master.

What had begun as tiny quivers of pleasure, quickly
built up into a powerful flood of sensation peaking in
intense shudders of delight that convulsed and
possessed her, her small cries of fulfilment blending

with the harsh, almost unfamiliar sound of Simon's
voice as his body shuddered almost violently into
release.

For a long time afterwards he simply held her in his
arms, murmuring soft sounds of comfort in her ear;
holding her, touching her until her body stopped
trembling and she was at last calm. When she felt able
to speak she said shakily, 'I never imagined . . . is it
always like that?' She tensed slightly, already
regretting her impulsive question. How naïve he
would think her, but instead of laughing or taunting
he said softly,

'Are you asking me to pass a general comment, or
give a personal opinion? If it's the former, then yes I
believe it can be given the right circumstances and the
optimum combination of need, desire and emotion,
but if it's the latter then no.' He had curled her into
his side, keeping her there with his arm, but now he
rolled towards her, his hand cupping her jaw, turning
her to face him. 'For me it's never been like that before. Good yes . . . even very good, but no other woman
has ever made me feel almost immortal.' A smile
curled his mouth as he added, almost self-derisively.
'That's what six years of frustration does for you.'

His cynical comment broke Christy's mood. By
saying that he had reminded her that all he felt for her
was desire. She wanted to move away from him and to
shut herself away somewhere to cry, but he was
holding her too tightly. 'Go to sleep.' His voice was
soft and faintly slurred, and as she made to pull away
from him, he snapped off the bedside lamp and said
slowly. 'No, stay here . . . Tonight I want you beside
me, Christy. Give me that at least.'

It was an odd thing for him to say when surely he must now be able to guess that there was precious little she would not give him. It amazed her that he still seemed not to have guessed how she felt about him; perhaps it was because *he* did not need love to experience desire. Sighing faintly Christy realised that he was already asleep. She couldn't be here when he woke up. She couldn't stay on in his apartment working for him, loving him, wanting him. Restless now and unable to sleep she slipped from the bed and went back to her own room.

She would have to leave. Driven by urgency now she pulled open cupboards and drawers, moving as quickly and quietly as she could as she stuffed her clothes haphazardly into her suitcases. It was only when she had finished that she realised she had nowhere to go. Her mother was away on holiday and she had no key to the house with her. Sighing in frustration she stared helplessly round the room. Where on earth could she go? Not to an hotel at this time of night, it was gone two in the morning . . . then where?

Suddenly it came to her. Miles. She could go to Miles!

Her cases weren't too heavy and she managed to get past Simon's door without waking him. For once luck seemed to be with her. The commissionaire on duty in the foyer seemed completely unsurprised when she told her halting story about a sick relative and asked him to get her a taxi. In the ten minutes it took for one to arrive she was almost sick with tension dreading Simon suddenly appearing in the foyer demanding to know where she was going, but he never did.

She gave the driver Miles' address and sank back in her seat wrapped in a miserable silence. Her earlier burst of tense energy seemed to have drained away leaving her almost exhausted and more unhappy than she could ever remember being before in her life.

Ringing Miles' bell half an hour later she began to panic. What if Miles had gone out again . . .? What if . . . She saw a light snap on upstairs and then five minutes later Miles opened the door, his hair tangled, his eyes crinkled with sleep.

'Christy!' When he realised who his visitor was he opened the door properly. 'God, I thought for one dreadful moment you were Imogen. Come on in.'

She followed him inside shaking with relief.

'Good heavens, what's the matter?'

She had followed Miles into his neat kitchen and now he was looking at her properly and could see the white tension of her face and the near exhaustion darkening her eyes.

'Miles . . . could I please stay here for tonight . . . I can't stay with Simon . . . Tomorrow I'll go home . . . The vicar always keeps a spare key but . . .'

'Christy . . . Christy, of course you can stay here.' His smile was wryly understanding. 'I won't ask what's wrong because I have a feeling I already know the answer, and besides it's none of my business. The spare room bed is always made up. I'll take you up there, and then I'll make you a hot drink, come on.'

Oh the relief of letting someone else take charge . . . of not having to think or worry. Even so, and despite Miles' warm drink, it seemed like hours before she finally managed to get to sleep, her body constantly feeding her with images of Simon . . . Simon . . . lying

in her arms ... making love to her ... touching her
... kissing her ... but at last she did sleep, waking late
in the morning, wondering for a few minutes exactly
where she was.

She showered and dressed reluctantly, wanting to
stay where she was as though by doing so she could
hide from herself and her own emotions.

When she went downstairs she could hear the clatter
of a typewriter from Miles' study, and knocked
hesitantly on the door. The noise stopped and the
door opened. Miles smiled in relief when he saw her.
'Hello, Sleeping Beauty,' he teased, 'I thought you
were going to sleep for ever. Feeling any better?' he
added awkwardly. 'Last night ...'

'I shouldn't have come here,' Christy apologised,
'but I just didn't know where to go ... I couldn't go
home ... and I couldn't stay with Simon. ...' She
shivered, and Miles covered her hands with his own.
'Of course you should have come here. We're friends
aren't we, Christy, and that's what friends are for.' A
tiny grin curled his mouth. 'I only wish that Imogen
had taken it into her head to come and visit me. It
might have convinced her that I don't want her. By
the way,' he added, 'there's a photograph and a couple
of lines about us in one of the morning papers, want to
see it?'

He searched around on his desk and then
brandished the newspaper. He had already opened it
on the appropriate page and Christy felt her stomach
clench as she looked into her own familiar features,
staring back at her from the paper. The photograph
had obviously been taken when they were dining
together, although there was no sign of Imogen.

'Writer Miles Trent dining with his recent assistant Christy Lawrence. Could romance be blossoming between this recently inseparable pair? Christy it will be remembered accompanied Miles to India last year while he was working on his bestselling novel *Mutiny*.'

'That should put her off the scent,' Miles announced with evident satisfaction. 'Her father's an extremely moral-toned man and once he thinks I'm involved with someone else, he'll soon put a stop to her antics.'

'I'd better make some arrangements for getting home,' Christy intervened. 'May I use your 'phone?'

'Why the rush? Your mother's away, why not stay here for a few days? I could do with some help to tidy up my correspondence.' He grinned to show that he was only joking. 'In fact,' he added on a more serious note, 'I'm supposed to be attending a publicity bash tonight. Why don't you come with me, it will do you good?'

'I didn't know you'd got anything new coming out?'

'I haven't. It's for one of my agent's new protegées, but he's invited as many well-known names as he can as well. Since he's my agent, I could hardly refuse. It will mean an overnight stay. He's got a huge sprawling place in Gloucestershire, so you needn't worry that there won't be room for you. In fact, if you fancy the idea, I'll give him a ring and warn him to expect you.'

She had never felt less in a party mood, but why not go? At least it would stop her from having too much time on her own to brood. If she went back to the vicarage that was exactly what she would do.

'Well, if you're sure you don't mind?'

'Mind ... Why should I? I *am* male enough to enjoy escorting a beautiful woman, Christy,' he told her drily.

A phone call to his agent confirmed that Christy would be welcome to accompany him and that there would be plenty of room for her. She would have to go out and buy something to wear, Christy reflected wryly. The blue silk, which would have been admirably suitable, was still no doubt lying on Simon's bedroom floor. What would his housekeeper make of that? Christy wasn't naïve enough to believe that she was the only woman who had ever shared Simon's bed; but she suspected she was certainly the only one who had left it in the middle of the night, leaving half her wardrobe behind.

Miles told her that he wanted to leave for Gloucestershire about four o'clock. It was gone ten now, but she had no appetite for food so she might as well go out and find something to wear.

It didn't take her long. She was in no mood for buying clothes, and the slim-fitting, dark navy, cream-speckled Caroline Charles silk suit she discovered in a Chelsea boutique seemed just the right choice for a publicity bash. In stark contrast to the blue silk, it buttoned primly up to the neck and had a delicate peter pan collar with matching cream cuffs. She looked like someone's secretary in it, she reflected cynically, wondering what the Press would make of the fact that Miles would be escorting her to the 'do'. What did it matter? Simon was hardly likely to be concerned who her name was coupled with. Simon! Treacherously her heart started to ache, her body shivering as she re-lived the touch of his hands upon it. Dear God, would it never end? Why ask; she already knew the answer to that one.

She got back to Miles' house in plenty of time for their departure. His agent's house was in the country he had said, which meant that it might be wise to take along some casual clothes. He had told her that they would probably stay over for lunch and then return, and she packed accordingly.

Miles' agent's house was a neo-Gothic Victorian monstrosity which he told her had caught the eye of his American wife, and which she had insisted on buying.

'Fortunately, it's extremely comfortable inside—its only saving grace,' Miles told her as he parked in front of the house. There were several other cars there already—an indication that they were not the first to arrive.

'You might find Charles a little over-ebullient,' Miles warned her as they went in. 'Pay no attention, it's just his way.'

They were greeted by their host and hostess almost immediately and Christy could see what Miles meant. Charles Orton was a tall, florid man in his late fifties, with thick silver-grey hair and sharp, faded blue eyes that took note of and obviously recognised her. His grip when he shook hands with her was firm to the point of being almost forceful, and he emanated a hearty sincerity which she suspected could be slightly overpowering.

His wife was one of that breed of American women who breathe money and all that it can buy. Beautifully slim, immaculately coiffured and made-up, she was elegance personified, Christy reflected, and could have been any age from thirty-five to forty-five. She was also extremely charming, her smile warm and welcoming as she shook Christy's hand.

'So you're Christy,' she exclaimed. 'We've heard so much about you, and of course Charles is a great admirer of your mother.' Christy gave a non-committal smile.

'Several other people have arrived, and we're just having an informal get together in the drawing room. I'll get the maid to take you up to your rooms and if you feel like joining us please do.'

'Thank you.' Christy smiled at her. 'It's very kind of you to make room for me like this at the last minute.'

'Not at all.' Her hostess's smile was curious. 'This is the first time Miles has ever brought a . . . friend with him to one of our "dos". I take it that . . . er . . . separate rooms?'

'Oh yes,' Christy hastily confirmed, adding firmly, 'Miles and I are only friends.'

Her hostess's attention was taken by some new arrivals, so she didn't reply, and Christy stifled a faint sigh as she followed the maid upstairs.

Miles raised his eyebrows. 'Not sorry you came are you?'

'No . . .' Poor Miles. He was doing his best to cheer her up and she was being nothing but a misery. What did it really matter if Charmaine Orton did draw the wrong conclusions about their relationship?

Her room was a pleasant one. Furnished with a double bed and decorated in soft, misty lilacs. There was a bathroom off it and a generously large wardrobe. Fresh flowers were arranged on the table in front of the mirror and there was also a large supply of engraved notepaper; some glossy magazines and an expensive tin of biscuits beside the bed.

Unwilling as yet to go down, Christy unpacked and re-did her make-up, debating whether it was best to change into her suit now, or wait until later. In the end thinking that a warm bath might relax her over-wound nerves, she decided that she might as well get ready now, rather than wait until later.

In the end it was almost two hours after her arrival before she eventually went downstairs again. The sound of voices coming from the drawing room confirmed that many more people had arrived during her absence, and she hesitated for a second by the open door, searching in vain for Miles' familiar fair head.

'Ah, Christy, my dear, there you are.' Charles Orton smiled at her warmly. 'Do come along in and meet some people. Miles has been button-holed by one of my American colleagues. He thinks Miles' latest book might make a good film.'

A little unwillingly Christie allowed herself to be drawn into the circles Charles had formed around himself. Some of the other guests she knew by sight; some to talk to. The publishing world was quite a small one, and she was familiar with these publicity 'dos' having attended several of them with her mother. She could see Miles now, pinned in a corner, listening to a small, bald-headed man who was talking earnestly to him. A small smile curved her mouth, and just as she was about to turn away her body froze. There, not three feet away from Miles, was Simon. And what was more he had seen her; seen her and was coming towards her. Sheer panic engulfed her. She turned

automatically to run, and found she could not, her
flight impeded by the other guests. Even so she
slipped hurriedly through the crowded room, intend
on gaining the safety of her bedroom. There had been
a look in Simon's eyes that warned her that he was not
in the best of moods; a look that warned her of the
inadvisability of letting him come any where near her.
He caught up with her just as she reached the door,
lean fingers curling round her wrist, his voice a harsh
sound in her ears as he said quietly, 'I want to talk to
you . . .'

'There's nothing to say.'

'No?'

He was standing close enough to her for her to see
the tawny gold flicker in his eyes; the glitter of intent
with which the hunter marked its prey and despite the
centrally heated warmth of the house she shivered.

'Why did you leave?'

People were looking covertly at them; all except
Miles who seemed to be too engrossed in his
conversation to see what was going on.

'People are staring . . .'

'Let them . . . or are you worried about what Trent
will say? Oh yes, I know that you went running to
him.' He practically snarled the words at her. She was
beginning to feel faint and decided that it must be
because of the torniquet like pressure his fingers were
applying to her arm.

'Simon . . . please . . . I feel faint . . .'

'Do you?' His mouth curled, and the glitter was now
burning into feral intent. 'How very Victorian of you,
but you won't escape me that way. You and I have to
talk . . .'

'There's nothing for us to talk about.'

'Isn't there . . .? What about the small matter of our contract; the fact that you agreed to work for me until my research was finished?'

Christy almost gasped. Surely he wouldn't want her to work for him now?

'What's the matter? Doesn't Trent want his woman working for another man? You gave me your virginity, Christy. Me!' He ground the words out thickly, his eyes never leaving her face, registering every small change of emotion. 'Yes, that's something you can't deny is it, no matter how much you might want to? Why did you? Didn't Trent want you as a virgin? He doesn't know what he's missed. Perhaps I ought to tell him.'

Christy had gone white. She couldn't speak for the pain lodged deep inside her body spreading tentacles out all over it, choking her . . . killing her . . .

'Ah Simon, you gorgeous man, there you are. You don't mind if I steal him away from you for a while do you, Christy?' Charmaine put her arm through Simon's smiling professionally at Christy. Mind? If only the other woman knew. She could tell that Simon did not want to go; that he hadn't finished with her, but already Charmaine was chattering away to him, making it easy for her to make her escape. She looked longingly into the garden. Her skin felt hot . . . too hot and she longed to breathe in fresh air. As she hovered uncertainly in the doorway a maid came in with a fresh tray of canapés. Christy stopped her and asked if there was any way she could get into the garden unobtrusively. She didn't want to use the main entrance and risk being seen by Simon, who would undoubtedly follow her, intent on further torment.

'There's some French windows in the sitting room, Miss,' the maid told her. 'They're normally unlocked. Are you feeling all right?' she added anxiously. 'If there's something I could get you?'

'No, I'm fine, just a little overheated.' Charmaine had obviously trained her staff well, and leaving the girl looking rather anxiously after her Christy followed her directions as to how she might find the sitting room.

The cool, fresh evening air was bliss against her burning skin. She wanted to walk and go on walking for ever; as though by doing so she might somehow escape from beneath the burden of her unwanted emotions. Simon here? That was the last thing she had thought of, but why not? After all he was as much a part of the publishing world as Miles ... Miles ... She hoped he wasn't worrying about her, but he had been so engrossed in his conversation she doubted that he had even realised she had gone.

She was a little surprised that Simon had guessed she had gone to Miles, but then of course she had allowed him to believe that she and Miles were romantically involved. Surely though it was stretching the imagination too far to suspect that he had come down here simply to seek her out? He could want to see her as little as she did him, although for far different reasons. She had left partially because she could not trust herself to stay without betraying her feelings and partially because she could not endure the thought of Simon believing she had made love with him using her virginity to trap him into a relationship he did not want, as he had accused her of trying to do in the past.

She shivered, suddenly realising that she was cold. For a perceptive man, Simon was behaving totally irrationally. Surely he himself must realise that it was better for her to leave? He didn't want any emotional involvement with her; he loved someone else. He had wanted her sexually yes, but to berate her with breaking their contract . . . She knew his work meant a lot to him, but surely not more than the risk of allowing her to become emotionally involved with him; not after what had happened when she was a teenager. The more she thought about his behaviour the less Christy understood it. He had behaved like a man consumed with a bitter need for vengeance . . . for vengeance against whom and for what?

Slowly she re-traced her steps. She should not have run away from him; she should have allowed him to talk . . . In fact she had been foolish to leave his apartment in the first place, the way that she had, but then she had acted on emotions alone. It wouldn't take a man of his acute perceptions long to realise why she had left, and perhaps then he would leave her alone. It was humiliating to think of him guessing how she felt about him, but she must have betrayed herself a thousand or more times by now. She really ought to talk to him; to explain rationally that she did not think it was wise for them to continue to work together. He would realise why, but she could not bring herself to do so yet.

She went back into the drawing room. Miles was standing just inside the door and he smiled at her, drawing her towards him.

'Where have you been? I was worried about you. Stay here and I'll go and get you a drink.'

'Worried, but not worried enough to come and find out where you were.' Simon's voice came from behind her, but she refused to turn round, fixing her eyes instead on Miles' retreating back . . . 'Is he really what you want Christy . . .?'

'Simon darling . . . How are you, it's been ages.'

She was racked with jealousy at the unmistakably sexual undertones to the woman's husky voice, but she didn't turn round. She couldn't. This was going to be the most awful evening. She wished she had never come.

By eleven o'clock her head was aching so badly she could scarcely endure the pain. She had hardly touched the food Miles had brought her from the buffet, and the champagne she had drunk had left her mouth dry and acid.

'Miles, if you don't mind, I think I'll go up to bed.'

'No, of course not.' He looked concerned. 'Can I get you anything? Charmaine might . . .'

'No . . . no . . .' Christy shook her head. 'It's just a headache, it will probably go when I lie down.'

'Just a headache?' His smile was wry. 'Oh, Christy, I think it's a little more than that. I've seen the way you've been watching Simon when you think no one's looking and the way he's been watching you. Do you love him?'

What could she say? 'I'm afraid so.'

'Umm. Love must surely be the most painful human emotional condition—and the most pleasurable. You go off to bed then. I want to have a chat with Charles, so I'll see you in the morning.'

Her room was a welcome haven of peace and silence. Her head ached so badly that all she wanted to do was to crawl into bed and lie there in the darkness, but first she had to undress and take off her make-up ... to shower and brush her hair. At last she was free to get into bed, but sleep had never seemed more elusive. She had some tablets in her handbag. Wearily she got up and went and got them, taking two and padding into the bathroom for a glass of water. The night was warm ... almost too warm, even though she had thrown open the windows. She pulled off her cotton nightdress and got back into bed, praying that tonight she would not dream about Simon. If she did, she didn't think she could endure it.

At last the pills started to do their work. She hovered on the edge of sleep for what felt like an aeon of time and then gradually slid into its welcoming black abyss.

CHAPTER TEN

A SMALL sound woke her, and she struggled to assimilate the import of it, still muzzy with sleep. What had it been? A click . . . a . . . a sound like someone opening a door? Her door? She felt too hazy to sit up and switch on her bedside lamp and so instead she called out huskily, 'Miles . . . is that you?'

It was like suddenly being confronted with an unexpected physical force, and being imprisoned by it. The lamp was snapped on, half blinding her with its unexpected brilliance. 'No, it damned well is not.'

Simon! Now the muzziness had gone and in its place was a flowering of such intense joy that she could scarcely contain it, until reality broke through destroying it. 'Simon, what are you doing here?' She clutched nervously at the sheet, remembering that she was wearing nothing beneath it, convinced that she had never looked worse; her hair a tangled mass and her face free of make-up.

'What do you think?'

'It's a bit late to talk about the contract.' She had no idea what time it was and even as she said the words they struck her as ludicrous. Simon obviously thought so too. 'What a little ostrich you are, Christy,' he mocked tauntingly. 'Why isn't Miles with you?'

His question caught her off-guard. 'I . . . had a headache . . . I came to bed early.'

His smile was bitterly savage, with no warmth in it

whatsoever. She had never seen the golden eyes glow so coldly. 'Poor devil, he's getting the headache treatment already and you're not even married yet. You'll have to admit him to your bed sometime, Christy, otherwise what will you tell him if you find you're carrying my child, or isn't he man enough to care? He doesn't want you, Christie—not the way I want you, otherwise you'd never be sleeping here alone, but you already know that, don't you?'

'Please go away.'

His laughter jarred on her sensitive nerves. 'My, how polite we are.' His mouth twisted in an acid smile. 'Almost as polite as you were the other night. "Please make love to me Simon,"' he whispered mockingly, imitating her, bringing back images she had thought successfully banished, '"please, please Simon . . ."'

'Stop it . . . stop it.' She had her hands over her ears, but he sat down on the bed and wrenched them away, gripping her wrists almost painfully as he forced her arms down. 'Do you beg him to make love to you?' he demanded savagely, '*Do you?*'

All she could do was shiver, and shake her head.

'Do you know why I've come here tonight, Christy?' His thumb was rubbing hypnotically against the fast pulse beating in her wrist, soothing and yet inflaming her. She felt curiously weak as though her bones were melting; as though his touch was slowly robbing her of all her ability to resist him.

'To discuss our contract.'

The topaz eyes glittered. 'Wrong,' he said softly, 'This was why I came.'

The hard pressure of his mouth on hers stunned her. She made an inarticulate protest beneath it,

tensing her body, but his torso was pinning her to the
bed, and his fingers were still locked round her wrists.
Now his mouth was moving slowly over hers, teasing,
tormenting ... knowing just how to undermine her
defences. He released her wrists but instead of
pushing him away, her arms locked round him, and
suddenly she was responding helplessly to the warm
pressure of his mouth, accepting and then returning it,
her lips moving against his, parting eagerly to admit
the driving force of his tongue. Lost in the surge of
longing only he could arouse in her, she wasn't even
aware of him tugging down the sheet until she felt his
hands on her body and by then it was far too late to
even think of stopping him.

When they had made love before she had had only
instinct and love to guide her, now to those she could
add knowledge—the knowledge of how to please and
arouse him and she wanted to do both. So much that
the tiny voice inside her that warned she was courting
danger was silenced without even being heard. Simon
was fully dressed, but although her fingers trembled
occasionally over buttons and fastenings, he made no
move to help her, simply watching her from between
slitted eyelids, touching her so that she ached for the
act of consumation. It seemed a lifetime before they
were both naked and she was free to touch his skin, to
shower him with kisses and to stroke feverish hands
over the satin flesh that cloaked steel muscles.

'You want me ... let me hear you say it.' There was
arrogant sureness in his voice and something else ...
something that aroused vague memories but remained
tantalisingly elusive. She ought to deny it, but what was
the point; he must know by now how she felt about

him; her touch, her need alone must surely have betrayed her, and surely he must care something for her to have come to her? Surely it could not simply be because he resented her going to Miles? It was as though someone had poured ice down her spine. Her body tensed and froze. Fool, fool she berated herself, of course it was exactly that. Simon didn't care about her; he simply wanted to reinforce his domination to her. Six years ago he had rejected her and he would reject her again.

'What's wrong?' He had picked up on her tension and his hands ceased their seductive movement against her skin. It was nearly killing her to do it, but she must make him leave her room before it was too late and before she betrayed herself completely.

'I want you to leave.'

She heard him swear and winced slightly. 'Like hell you do,' he told her thickly. 'You want me to stay. You want me . . .'

'Just because we've made love once, it doesn't necessarily mean I want to repeat the experience.' She made herself sound cold and uncaring, hardly daring to believe she had actually deceived him, but she must have done because she felt his faint withdrawl.

'No?'

She couldn't see his face because he had moved out of the light, but his voice was all smooth disbelief. Like the jungle panther he was at his most dangerous when he purred, Christy thought achingly, and she would have to be on her guard.

'Are you trying to tell me that you'd rather have Miles here in your bed?'

What could she say; how could she defend herself

against him? Suddenly it came to her. 'He at least wants to marry me.' Her heart was pounding desperately, the tension in the silence that followed her words making her throat ache.

'And marriage is what you want?'

She essayed a brief shrug. 'I haven't changed that much in six years.' Would he believe her? It seemed impossible that he could and she could feel his eyes resting on her, assessing her. If anything could kill his desire it must be this.

'And when you let me make love to you was it because you thought I might marry you?'

She would have to be careful here. She forced her voice to sound cool. 'Of course not. I already knew you would not.'

'So then why?'

She gave another shrug. 'I seem to remember you said I owed it to you . . . perhaps I felt I ought to pay off all my old debts . . .'

The silence was hideously taut, and then she heard him swear and cringed from the violence in his voice. Quite what she might have said Christy never knew because totally unexpectedly her bedroom door opened and Miles walked in, snapping on the main light. Of the three of them he was probably the least surprised, Christy realised later. He had obviously not yet been to bed, but he did look tired.

'I was on my way up and I thought I'd come in and see how you were.'

Christy stifled an hysterical urge to laugh, laughter turning to shock as Simon reached out and pulled her hard against him beneath the covers, his mouth warm against her ear as he said quite audibly. 'Well, my love, here's your chance to tell him.' When she made no move to speak he said curtly, 'I'm sorry you had to find out like this, Miles, but Christy has decided she prefers me.'

Christy saw Miles blink and thought it was no wonder ... She half expected him to make some remark that would betray her, but instead he responded equably. 'Er ... yes ... so I see. I'll bid you both good night.'

When he had gone and the room was once again softened into shadowy lamplight Christy hissed furiously. 'Why did you have to say that, now he'll ...'

'He'll what? Realise that we're lovers? So what, we are aren't we? He hardly appeared unduly concerned, for a man who's supposed to be marrying you.'

Suddenly it was all too much for her. Tears spurted weakly in her eyes and dripped betrayingly on to Simon's hand. 'But why ... what possible reason could you have for behaving like this, Simon?'

His laugh was completely mirthless. 'One of the strongest known to man. Love!' He saw her expression and laughed again. 'Don't look at me like that. Surely you've guessed. In fact I believe once I actually told you.'

'You said there was someone you loved,' Christy agreed slowly, 'but I never imagined it was me. How could I after the way you rejected me six years ago?'

'Look ...' he grasped her upper arms, half shaking her, 'I rejected you, as you call it, then because I had no other alternative.

'I wanted you then, Christy and very badly, but I wasn't ready for the sort of permanent relationship you had in mind. You were so young and idealistic. The intensity of your commitment to me scared me half to death. There were so many things I wanted to see and do, and it wasn't just that. I knew I was already half way in love with you then, and I also knew that you were far too young to weather the potential storms there were bound to be; storms you couldn't see at all, and that I could see too well. I suspect it was simply that there was too much blind faith on your part and too little on mine. I thought you were too young to really know your own heart. I love you, Christy, I always have. Not perhaps after the fashion of a knight on a white charger; not like the hero of a romance, but very deeply for all that; far too much to trap you in a marriage I felt sure you'd be regretting within twelve months.'

'And now?'

It was too much for her to take in all at once; too much of a shock for her to be able to believe what he was saying.

'And now I still love and want you. Enough to be sure we could have something together you could never have with Miles.'

'You mean sex?'

'I mean this.' He leaned over and kissed her slowly, until her body surged mindlessly against his. 'Call it by whatever name you choose, nothing can diminish its power can it?' he asked softly.

Christy couldn't trust herself to believe what he was saying. He *couldn't* love her. It was all a trick, although why he should want to trick her in such a cruel fashion she didn't know.

'Passion means nothing. It will fade.'

'Will it?' He shifted his weight across her body and in the moonlight she saw his grim smile. 'My passion for you as you call it, hasn't faded in six years. If anything I love and want you more now than I did then.'

'Enough to marry me?'

She could feel him watching her. 'You'd better believe it,' he told her softly.

'This wouldn't be some sort of trick to get me to admit that I still love you would it, Simon?'

He swore briefly and then shook her. 'Christ, Christy, can't you differentiate between lust and love? Can't you tell how I feel about you? Let's stop fighting and be honest with one another for a change. I love you and I always have. Nothing can change that, Christy, whether you love me in return or not. If you love me, you're going to have to take me on trust. It works both ways you know,' he told her wryly. 'I've been hurting like hell myself listening to you saying you merely "want" me; having you throw your relationship with Miles in my face. Finding out that you were still a virgin. How the hell do you think that made me feel? Oh I knew I'd hurt you—I had to, I had no choice, but I never wanted to hurt you to the extent that you'd wall your emotions and feelings completely away.'

'I apologise if my virgin state upset you.'

She knew her voice sounded tight and strained.

'Upset me! Christ, have you listened to *anything* I've said?' Simon sounded angry now, really angry. 'Of course it damned well didn't upset me. I love you, Christy, and discovering that I would be your first lover was like ... oh I don't know ... an alcoholic suddenly coming across a cellar full of vintage wines.

What upset me was knowing how deeply I'd hurt you, and yet I wouldn't have been human if part of me didn't rejoice in the fact that you'd known no other man. I'd have told you I loved you then but you've fought me every step of the way ... prickly and defensive as a little hedgehog.'

Christy opened her mouth to speak but he silenced her. 'Yes. I know you've had good reason. I know there's no reason on earth why you should return my love, and if you turned me down now and told me to get the hell out of your life, it would be no more than I deserved, but I did it partially for you as well. You were too young for marriage then, or at least the sort of marriage I could have given you ... but I always intended to come back for you, given half the chance. When I read about you being in India with Miles last year, it took every ounce of willpower I possessed not to go out there and drag you away from him. Come on, gypsy lady,' he whispered softly, 'let's call a halt to the vendetta and be honest with one another.'

In the half-light Christie looked at him, longing to believe him and yet still half afraid to do so ... too much had happened too soon, turning over all her preconceived ideas and beliefs. She reached out to touch him and felt his body clench beneath her hand. For the first time he allowed her to see into his eyes without guarding or shielding his expression, and joy burst gloriously into flower inside her, as she realised that he was telling the truth; that he did love her. Of course there had been signs she had been too blind and stubborn to see ... little things.

'Christy ... I can't wait much longer.' His plea was a husky reminder of what she was withholding from him. She smiled into his eyes and let her fingertips caress him.

'I love you, Simon.' She whispered the words against his mouth, sensing his tension, feeling it turn into joy. 'Say it again,' he muttered against her mouth. 'Tell me again . . .'

'I love you, I love you, I love you. . .'

'Umm. I begin to get the message.' He pressed her back against the bed kissing her passionately, not seeking to hide from her the effect she had on him.

He had hurt her, and she had sworn never to forgive him for it with all the vehement passion of a spurned teenager, but what he had said to her tonight had held an unmistakable ring of truth; she *had* been too young . . . too young and idealistic to adapt to his way of life which she knew for the last few years had involved constant absences abroad, tours, lectures . . . long periods when he had shut himself away to write. At eighteen could she have coped with that?

On a long sigh she admitted inwardly that she could not and that he had perhaps made the wisest decision. And he, too, had suffered. She could see that now, taste it in the taut passion of his kiss; in the way his hands moved over her body as though they could not get enough of her.

'What would you have done if I had denied that I loved you?'

She felt him smile against her skin. 'Kept on trying until I was convinced there was no hope left, and I felt sure there was hope; the mere fact that you allowed me to persuade you to come and work for me proved that. Speaking of which,' he twisted one long curl idly round his finger, tugging gently on her scalp, 'I heard from the Admiralty today ... that jug you brought up from the sea bed is silver-gilt and what's more it's engraved. ...'

Excitement spiralled headily inside her. 'What does it say?'

'It says ...' and his mouth was almost against her own. 'To my beloved husband Kit.'

'Then it's true ... The legend is true ...'

'Based on truth at least.'

'And you'll write the book.'

'Only if you agree to marry me. St Paul's would make an ideal spot for a honeymoon, don't you agree?'

'And if I don't?'

'Well then I'll just have to hold you to our contract and take you there anyway. Who knows, given time and an endless supply of seductive tropical nights I might ... just might be able to change your mind. I played my last card when I tricked you into agreeing to work for me, Christy,' he told her more soberly. 'You had every reason to loathe and resent me I know that, but believe me I did what I did because I thought it was best. Six years ago neither of us had the maturity to build a solid lasting marriage.'

'And now?'

'Now I believe we both have, but the decision must be yours. I want it all ... marriage ... a home ... children ... but most of all you ... you. Sharing my life ... my bed ... my hopes and my fears. Well?'

Although he sounded relaxed Christie knew better and her heart ached with love for him. Yes he had hurt her, but he had been hurt himself; he had acted as he thought best, making a decision for them he felt her too young to take. It would have been so easy for him to make love to her and then reject her, but he had not done so. He had left her free to find someone else.

Against his mouth she murmured the words, 'How soon can we be married? Because this time I don't intend to let you go.'

'Come on.'

To her surprise he threw back the covers and started hunting round for his clothes.

Christy stared at him perplexed. 'What are you doing?'

'Getting dressed and so are you. I want to make love to you, but when I do I want to be sure that we aren't going to be interrupted. You and I are going back to London, and then I'm going to chain you to my side to make sure this time when I wake up I don't wake up alone.'

'Mum's going to be surprised when she gets back,' Christy reflected.

'You think so?' Simon stopped dressing long enough to grin at her.

'You mean she knew?'

'I had to tell her before she would agree to let me approach you about working for me. It was my last chance. I was scared stupid I would lose you to Miles, and it was the best method of keeping you away from him that I could come up with, but don't expect me to wait until she comes home to marry you. The three days it takes to get a special licence is more than long enough.' He took her in his arms and kissed her, frowning slightly when she pulled away, his frown changing to a mocking smile when she asked breathlessly, 'How long does it take to get back to London?'

Coming Next Month in Harlequin Presents!

855 A FOREVER AFFAIR Rosemary Carter
Despite its savage beauty, her husband's African game reserve is
no longer home. Was it carved in stone that she could never love
another man? Surely a divorce would change that!

856 PROMISE OF THE UNICORN Sara Craven
To collect on a promise, a young woman returns her talisman—
the protector of virgins—to its original owner. The power of the
little glass unicorn was now with him!

857 AN IRRESISTIBLE FORCE Ann Charlton
A young woman is in danger of being taken over by a subtle
irresistible force rather than by open aggression when she takes
on an Australian construction king who's trying to buy out her
grandmother.

858 INNOCENT PAWN Catherine George
Instead of looking past the money to the man behind it, a mother
is prompted by panic to blame her husband when their five-year-
old daughter is kidnapped.

859 MALIBU MUSIC Rosemary Hammond
California sunshine and her sister's beach house provide the
atmosphere a young woman needs to focus on her future—until
her neighbor tries to seduce her.

860 LADY SURRENDER Carole Mortimer
The man who bursts into her apartment can't see why his best
friend would throw away his marriage for a woman like her. But
soon he can't imagine any man—married or otherwise—*not*
falling for her.

861 A MODEL OF DECEPTION Margaret Pargeter
A model takes on an assignment she can't handle when she tries
to entice a man into selling his island in the Caribbean. She was
supposed to deceive the man, not fall in love.

862 THE HAWK OF VENICE Sally Wentworth
Most people travel to Venice to fall in love. Instead, an au pair girl
makes the journey to accuse a respected Venetian count of
kidnapping—or of seduction, at least.

SPECIAL FREE OFFER

Janet Dailey

TREASURY EDITION

- *NO QUARTER ASKED*
- *FIESTA SAN ANTONIO*
- *FOR BITTER OR WORSE*

Now's your chance to rediscover your favorite Janet Dailey romance characters – Cord and Stacey Harris, and Travis McCrea.

Own three Janet Dailey novels in one deluxe hardcover edition. A beautifully bound volume in gold-embossed leatherette… an attractive addition to any home library.

Here's how to get this special offer from Harlequin!

SEPTEMBER
TREASURY EDITION
COUPON

As simple as 1…2…3!

1. Each month, save one Treasury Edition coupon from your favorite Romance or Presents novel.
2. In four months you'll have saved four Treasury Edition coupons (<u>only one coupon per month allowed</u>).
3. Then all you have to do is fill out and return the order form provided, along with the four Treasury Edition coupons required and $1.00 for postage and handling.

Mail to: Harlequin Reader Service

In the U.S.A.
2504 West Southern Ave.
Tempe, AZ 85282

In Canada
P.O. Box 2800, Postal Station A
5170 Yonge Street
Willowdale, Ont. M2N 6J3

RT1-B-2

Please send me my FREE copy of the Janet Dailey Treasury Edition. I have enclosed the four Treasury Edition coupons required and $1.00 for postage and handling along with this order form.

(Please Print)

NAME_____

ADDRESS_____

CITY_____

STATE/PROV._____ZIP/POSTAL CODE_____

SIGNATURE_____

This offer is limited to one order per household.

SUPPLIES LIMITED

This special Janet Dailey offer expires January 1986.

Just what the woman on the go needs!

BOOKMATE

The perfect "mate" for all Harlequin paperbacks!

Holds paperbacks open for hands-free reading!

- • TRAVELING
- • VACATIONING
- • AT WORK • IN BED
- • COOKING • EATING
- • STUDYING

Perfect size for all standard paperbacks, this wonderful invention makes reading a pure pleasure! Ingenious design holds paperback books OPEN and FLAT so even wind can't ruffle pages—leaves your hands free to do other things. Reinforced, wipe-clean vinyl-covered holder flexes to let you turn pages without undoing the strap...supports paperbacks so well, they have the strength of hardcovers!

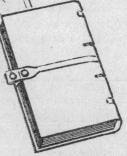

Snaps closed for easy carrying.

Available now. Send your name, address, and zip or postal code, along with a check or money order for just $4.99 + .75* for postage & handling (for a total of $5.74) payable to Harlequin Reader Service to:

Harlequin Reader Service

In the U.S.A.
2504 West Southern Ave.
Tempe, AZ 85282

In Canada
P.O. Box 2800, Postal Station A
5170 Yonge Street,
Willowdale, Ont. M2N 5T5

MATE-1R